WHO DO YOU TRUST?

by David Kippen

Back In The Nest

MANDY CAMERON was reaping the rewards of years of study and hard work. She'd joined a big Melbourne commercial law firm as a junior solicitor after graduating dux of her university class five years ago.

"We're so proud of you, darling," her parents had said when, just before Christmas, the case she'd been working on with the senior partner all last year was finally settled in favour of their client, a major pharmaceutical company.

Her role had been recognised, praised and

rewarded with promotion. Mandy's career prospects were bright.

She should have been happy and even excited to be moving smoothly along her chosen life's path. Yet the expected sense of fulfilment and satisfaction wasn't there.

Something was missing.

Maybe the problem was that success at school, at university and now in her job had always come to her without any real challenges apart from the usual need for dedication and hard work.

She was often referred to as "the smart one", "the talented one" or "the lucky one" whose parents could afford to support her through five years of university.

But today, sitting in the kitchen of her parents' comfortable home in Melbourne's leafy eastern suburbs where she and two older brothers had grown up, the usually bubbly twenty-nine-year-old was quiet.

"I guess I am a bit tired."

Mandy turned to the picture window that framed the swimming-pool and the large, tree-shaded backyard.

"Last year was so busy and then being forced out of my apartment by that fire was the last straw."

Merrill Cameron passed her daughter a coffee, noting her face was drawn with dark circles hanging heavy under her eyes.

"You need a proper holiday, love, not just a day or two off here and there."

"I know, Mum. But it's been difficult. Now that big case is settled it should be easier and I'll take some time off. Honest."

Mandy toyed with her cup.

"Anyway, I enjoyed our shopping today. I think those clothes we bought for your big trip really suit you!"

The attempt to divert her mother failed.

"That's good, love." Merrill pursed her lips. "What with all your work and then Jason going off like that you should get away from it all for a while.

"I had hopes for you and Jason." She clearly wanted to say more.

"Mum, I've told you before, Jason is a good friend but not my boyfriend."

This was true, however Mandy had hoped that, given time, her relationship with the talented, charismatic young doctor might grow into something more than friendship.

Her hopes were dashed last November after they'd enjoyed a day together at the Melbourne Cup.

On that spring evening, over drinks in a quiet bar, Jason told her he planned to accept the position he'd been offered with a Pacific Island missionary group.

Mandy was disappointed but not greatly surprised – she'd known for some time about his interest in the position.

Despite his promising career prospects Jason was disillusioned with the city rat race, as he called it.

"What about your career?" she exclaimed. "All your study and hard work is starting to pay off now you've finally landed your dream position at the Royal Melbourne Hospital."

"I know some people will say I'm silly and it won't do my career prospects any good," he replied calmly. "Be that as it may, this is a chance to use my training and skills to make a real difference for real people, rather than just continue up the career tree here."

Make a real difference for real people.

Mandy still mused over those words. Her firm's corporate clients spent big money and she invested a lot of time in their cases, but they weren't real people. In fact they were quite impersonal.

A vehicle pulled into the yard, rousing her.

"Look, your father's got it!" Merrill announced, her face beaming.

Mandy saw a big, new, shiny silver SUV from which a well-built man was alighting.

Clive Cameron smiled and waved as he walked toward the house, his firm step and upright bearing proving his recent health scare was now history.

Mandy and her mother hurried out to greet him and to admire the new vehicle.

"Isn't she a beauty?" Clive enthused.

If she ever married she hoped it would turn out as well for her, Mandy decided, watching her parents.

They were like a pair of young lovers planning their honeymoon as they chatted and laughed about their forthcoming caravan trip around Australia to celebrate their 40th wedding anniversary.

The trip, originally scheduled for next year, had been brought forward.

Clive's health scare had made him conclude that opportunities not taken when available might well be missed.

Once his doctors had cleared him he had taken early retirement from his senior management role at a large bank and, together with Merrill, had begun planning the trip.

The new vehicle suitably admired, they returned to the kitchen where Clive put the kettle on. Merrill set out freshly baked scones with jam and cream for afternoon tea.

"So, what's the plan now you're about to start the big adventure?" Mandy put her empty cup down and turned to her parents, smiling.

"We're ready, willing and able," Clive told

her heartily. "I'll pick up the caravan next week.

"Then a couple of weeks should see everything organised and after that we'll be away.

"That should give Bill and Mary enough time to arrange to house-sit for us while we're away."

"I'm so pleased. Uncle Bill and Auntie Mary are my favourite uncle and aunt!

"It will be fun living with them for a while, but after that I'll need to find another place of my own.

"I really appreciate you taking me in at short notice after that fire forced everybody out of my apartment building, but it's time for me to fly the nest again," Mandy concluded.

"I agree," Clive told her. "Much as we love having you here, young people need to get out and be independent, stand on their own two feet."

Mandy reflected on her father's words, little knowing how soon they would impact on her life.

Aunt Clara's Will

HELLO, Celia!" Merrill opened the front door to Mandy's work colleague and friend one evening a few days later. "Come in and take a seat.

"Mandy should be back soon. She has good news, but she can tell you herself."

A few minutes later Mandy came in.

"Well?" Celia was bursting with curiosity.

"What?" Mandy replied mischievously.

"Your good news!"

Mandy showed Celia a letter she'd received that day.

Dear Ms Cameron,

Re The Estate of Clara Isabell Cameron, deceased, late of Kalgoorlie Western Australia.

We act for the above estate and advise that after due investigation we confirm that you are the principal beneficiary of Miss Cameron's will.

Please find enclosed details of the estate. Contact us with your instructions . . .

"Your aunt Clara! That is good news," Celia exclaimed. "That'll get you another place to live. You could even buy one of those new apartments around Docklands and be a real city girl.

"Wait, though." Celia's lawyer's mind took over. "What about your brothers? Won't they feel left out if you get all your aunt's estate?"

"Thankfully, no. When she won Tattslotto a few years ago she gave them each a hefty deposit to buy a house.

"Because I was younger and still living at home it was agreed that I'd get my share when she passed on."

"That's good," Celia replied. "Squabbles over wills can get nasty."

"No worries there, but I do want to consider all my options," Mandy said thoughtfully. "And now, thanks to dear old Aunt Clara, I've got more options. Actually she was Dad's auntie, my great-aunt."

"That's right." Clive had joined them. "She was my father's older sister."

"Here, Dad, show Celia." Mandy picked up a photo album from the coffee table. "Dad has been showing us some family history."

Clive opened the album to an old black and white picture of three teenagers.

"That's Clara with my father and their older brother, William. He was always known as 'Bluey' because of his red hair."

Clive pointed to another old photo of two smiling, fresh-faced young men in army uniforms.

"That's Bluey and his mate, Curley Jackson. They met in the Army. Apparently they were characters, always in scrapes. Just like the larrikins in the 'Bluey And Curley' comics that were popular in the 1940s.

"This was taken before they were sent to New Guinea to repel the Japanese invasion."

"Sadly, neither of them returned," Mandy told Celia.

"Dad was too young to enlist until near the end of the war," Clive continued. "When he did finally enlist he was posted to Victoria where he met my mother. After the war they married and settled here.

"Clara never married. She stayed on in Kalgoorlie to look after their parents. When they died Dad invited her to Melbourne but she wanted to stay near all her friends."

"So she was the last Cameron in Kalgoorlie," Mandy added.

"That's sad," Celia said.

"Oh, we stayed in touch! Aunt Clara came over to visit us and we visited her. I had some great holidays in Kalgoorlie.

"Goodness, look at the time, Celia. We'd better get going." Mandy stood up.

"Enjoy the movie," Merrill said. "Don't forget you've got an early start tomorrow."

A City Girl?

NEXT morning Mandy set off early with Julian Adair, a senior partner in the legal firm where she worked.

They were going to Bendigo, 160 kilometres north of Melbourne, to gather information for an important case. They would need to stay overnight.

"I'm impressed with your work, Mandy, and I'm sure you have a bright future," Julian told her the following day as they drove back to Melbourne. "Your work on that pharmaceuticals case last year and now on this trip, has been first class.

"A word of advice – pace yourself. I know you're young and feel the need to prove yourself; that's admirable and to be encouraged.

"But take care you don't burn out. I've seen promising careers end that way."

"Thanks for your concern, Mr Adair. I suppose I have been pushing myself. There always seems to be so much to do!"

"Your dedication will help you succeed, Mandy, but you must look after yourself, too. Why don't you take some leave, to charge your batteries?

"The job will still be here when you get

back and you'll handle it all the better if you're refreshed."

"I plan to take Friday off. With the Australia Day holiday on Thursday I'll have a four-day weekend! My parents have suggested I join them for a short break while they try out their new caravan before they take off around Australia."

"Becoming grey nomads, are they?" Julian chuckled.

"I guess so. They plan to be away for about six months but this first trip will only be four days."

"That's a good start, but I think you should consider a longer holiday once this case is settled. And thanks to that information you unearthed we should be able to settle it quickly.

"Just remember what they say about all work and no play!"

Rounding a sweeping bend they found the traffic stopped. A large B-double truck with its two long trailers had demolished some 50 metres of the roadside wire barrier before it had run off the road and tipped over, spilling its load of boxes.

"I hope no-one's been hurt." Mandy surveyed the wreckage.

A police officer came up to Julian's window to advise.

"One lane should be open in about

twenty minutes once VicRoads have cleared the way."

He assured Mandy the driver was unhurt.

"Poor devil," Julian commented. "These interstate truckies are pushed to the limit with long hours and almost impossible schedules. Then, when something goes wrong, they're the ones in trouble while the bosses who push them escape unscathed.

"Work isn't everything," he concluded reflectively. "Maybe I should take my own advice and slow up while I can. Anyway, on a more positive note, where are you off to this weekend?"

"A little place called Whixley. We sometimes had family holidays there when my brothers and I were young.

"We'd stay in an old country pub. Nothing flash – it had shared bathroom and toilet facilities – but it was fun.

"Whixley was a quiet little town then but I haven't been back there for years. Dad liked to get away from the city 'rush and crush', as he put it, and have family time together.

"He was right. I really enjoyed those times to unwind, especially when I was under pressure preparing for exams."

"Whixley – isn't that somewhere around here?" Julian fiddled with the car's GPS. "Yes, there it is, about ten kilometres up ahead, just off the freeway. We can stop

there for lunch, if you like. Give you a
chance to see how it looks these days."

Forty minutes later Julian parked his silver-
grey BMW outside the Commercial Hotel in
Whixley's main street.

"I'm getting too old for these trips!"
Julian stretched the travel stiffness from his
body. "Any recommendation for where we
should eat?"

Mandy gazed around doubtfully.

"I'm not sure. Things have changed since I
was last here.

"There are all those new lots we passed,
where the farms have been subdivided."
She pointed across the road. "And the
Railway Hotel used to be a rundown dump
but now it looks quite upmarket!

"When we used to come here there were
only the two pubs, a general store and a
couple of others, plus the farm supply place
at the end of the street. Now there's that
mini-mart and several other new shops.

"There's even a law practice!" Mandy
exclaimed, indicating the sign a little way
along on the other side of the street.
"'Frank Barty, B.Com, LLB. Barrister &
Solicitor'," she read.

"Rather different from ours," Julian
remarked. "Probably just one practitioner
who'd have to deal with a wide variety of
cases. No room for a specialist firm here,

just basic legals for ordinary people."

"Making a real difference for real people?" Mandy asked thoughtfully.

"Yes, and that's important." Julian sounded wistful. "I admire anyone who takes on that sort of practice. The individual cases aren't as complex as ours, but the variety of law and being on your own must be challenging.

"You'd really have to stand on your own two feet."

"Real differences for real people," Mandy repeated.

Turning, she collided with a man who was hurrying by, making him drop his briefcase which sprang open, spilling papers over the footpath. His exclamation of annoyance was quickly followed by an apology.

"I'm so sorry!" Mandy helped retrieve his spilled papers.

With the papers safely collected he extended his hand.

"Steve Jackson. I hope you're not hurt."

"No," Mandy replied, smiling. "I'm Mandy Cameron and this is Mr Adair."

"Pleased to meet you. Excuse me, I'm late for an important appointment."

Mandy watched him hurry along the street to the bank.

He was about thirty with wavy red hair. His tanned face and arms indicated he worked outdoors.

He was probably a farmer or maybe a tradie supervisor from one of the building sites on the new lots on the way into town.

Was it a loan or some other problem that was taking him to the bank, she wondered.

As she watched he looked back. To her surprise her heart gave a little flip as their eyes met and he smiled before he entered the bank.

"Stop acting like a silly teenager," she silently chided herself. She forced her attention back to Julian who was speaking.

"About six months ago a couple of our friends decided to make a tree change so they bought a few hectares and moved to the country.

"They tell me it only takes an hour to get into the city on one of the new trains and they can work on their computers while they travel. Sounds a lot better than being stuck in traffic or on an overcrowded suburban train.

"I'd consider moving myself except I'd never get my wife out of Melbourne. She's a city girl." His voice was tinged with regret.

Was she a city girl? Mandy asked herself as they went into the Commercial Hotel for lunch.

Not A Nice Man

STEVE, come in. I've ordered coffee. White and one for you, isn't it?" The bank manager squinted through his wire-rimmed glasses.

Paul Robbins was a mousey man with a narrow sallow face.

He was unhappy and bitter, having realised, in his late fifties that managing a small country branch was as high as he'd ever climb on the banking corporate tree.

"Put it there!" he snapped as the junior teller brought their coffees in. "Careful!"

The tray wobbled as she tried to find space on his untidy desk and coffee slopped into a saucer when she jumped at his tone.

"Sorry," she stammered.

"No worries," Steve said, picking up the cup in question and smiling at the obviously upset girl who scuttled away.

"Sorry about that, Steve," Paul said in a very different tone of voice. "Got to keep on top of the staff."

He picked up his coffee and took a sip.

"She actually makes quite good coffee. Now, about your loan application. It's all in order so I can't see any problem with extending your overdraft."

"That's a relief. It's good to have a friendly bank manager when farming has been so tough, what with the dry seasons and all.

"Now I can build those covered cattle yards for my Wagyu Beef project and maybe look to buy some purebred stock."

"Always glad to help our oldest customers," Paul replied with a smile and handed the papers over for Steve to sign. "I've heard about Wagyu beef, but exactly what is it?"

Steve put down his pen and pushed the papers back to Paul.

"Wagyu are a Japanese cattle breed. The special thing about them is the way their meat is marbled with fat.

"The Japanese pay big money for that and now more and more local restaurants are also paying premium prices."

"I bet they charge their customers premium prices, too," Paul guessed.

"They sure do." Steve smiled. "But that means better prices for the farmer."

"And it makes it easier for you to repay your loan."

"In the long run, that's true. Meantime I'll have to be careful until it's all in place and my investment starts to pay."

Their business concluded, Steve stood to leave. He extended a hand to Paul who came around the desk to see him out.

"The Jacksons of Coolabah Flats were one of our first customers when this bank opened back in the pioneer days." Paul spoke in a honeyed, nasal tone.

"I trust we'll continue to serve you as well as the new customers we're getting now Larry Lawson is doing those farm sub-divisions.

"He's bringing a lot of new money and people to the district which can only be good for the town," he added.

At the same time Paul Robbins wished these newcomers would move their business to his bank rather than continue to deal with their city banks.

Maybe, then, he wouldn't be so reliant on Larry Lawson whose business was welcome but came at a price.

"I have mixed feelings about Larry Lawson and his dealings," was Steve's reply.

* * * *

On his way out Steve noticed the junior teller was almost in tears as Paul berated her again over the coffee.

"Bullies those who can't fight back and crawls to the rest. Not a nice man," he told himself.

"I wouldn't trust him as far as I could kick him, but you can't chip your bank manager when your overdraft is being approved!"

Best Of Both Worlds

THAT caravanning course was worthwhile,"
Clive said proudly as he surveyed the big
caravan now neatly parked on their site in
the Whixley Caravan Park.

"I'll pop the kettle on," Merrill said,
stepping into the van. "We've time for a
cuppa and a rest before lunch."

Two hours later they sat in the
Commercial Hotel dining-room.

"Still the same good old, country pub
meal!" Clive moved aside his empty plate.

The handsome, dark-haired waiter came
to clear the table and check everything was
to their satisfaction.

"Are you folk buying into one of those
new sub-divisions?" he asked with a
friendly smile. "The town has really kicked
on since Larry Lawson set up shop here."

"No, we're here for the weekend," Merrill
replied. "We've certainly noticed some
changes, though. We used to stay here
years ago for family holidays."

"Here at the Commercial?" The waiter
took a closer look at the Camerons.

"Yes," Merrill replied. "Of course, our
sons, Stuart and Greg, were with us then.

Now they're off with their own families.

The waiter's face lit up.

"You must be the Camerons!" He grinned. "I'm Brian."

Mandy's brothers and Brian Shelton, son of the proprietors of the Commercial Hotel, had been holiday mates all those years ago.

Thirteen-year-old Mandy had tagged along with them, dreaming of handsome Brian, but he'd never appeared to see her as anything more than his mates' kid sister.

"Dad and Mum are pretty much retired," Brian added. "I run the pub now. We kept it pretty traditional but we've started adding en-suite facilities to our guestrooms.

"Meanwhile Larry Lawson has made the Railway upmarket. But that's OK, there's plenty of room for both pubs with Larry bringing in all these new people.

"Let me know when you'll be in again. I'm sure Dad and Mum would love to say hello," he said as the Camerons left.

"No doubt about it, this Larry Lawson has brought a lot of change," Clive observed later as they ambled around town. "But Whixley still has that country feel."

They spent the next couple of days relaxing and exploring before heading back to Melbourne on Sunday.

While her parents chatted on the front seat Mandy reflected on her weekend.

Whitley definitely had its attractions and a plan was evolving in her mind.

Her dream job wasn't as dreamy as it had once been and her social life was nothing to write home about since Jason had left.

Maybe moving would help her find a way to make a real difference for real people, to find a purpose in life.

It was no longer enough for her to be just a cog in a corporate machine. She was determined to make some changes.

* * * *

One Friday in February, three weeks after her Whixley trip, Mandy and some colleagues were leaving the large Central Melbourne law firm where they worked.

They headed to the bar where they often went after a hectic work day, to unwind before facing the rush and crush home.

"Phew, it's hot! Forty-two degrees, I heard on the radio earlier, and the same predicted for the next few days," Mandy remarked. "Talk about a rat race," she added as they pushed through the milling crowd.

Although she'd been born and raised in Melbourne and had what some would call a dream job, Mandy was about to spring a surprise on her friends.

"Ah, that's better," Carl pronounced as they left the sweltering street for the air conditioned comfort of the bar.

A tall young man with dark hair, a clipped beard and black eyes, he was a couple of years ahead of Mandy and Celia in seniority and was building a promising legal career.

"What are we drinking?" He collected the group's orders before he and Mandy went to fetch the drinks.

"A little birdie tells me the big boss is very impressed with your work up in Bendigo and on that Big Pharma case," Carl said as they waited at the bar. "Congratulations, your dedication is paying off."

"Thanks. These big cases are very interesting and challenging, but lately they don't seem to give me any satisfaction."

"I guess we all get browned off at times," Carl replied as he paid for the drinks. "Maybe you need a holiday. I know I do!"

They carried the drinks back to where the other four had found a table in the crowded room and they all began to discuss their plans for the weekend.

An hour passed, then Celia stood up.

"See you all on Monday. If I don't go now I'll miss my train and the next one doesn't connect with the bus."

"You won't be seeing Mandy for a couple of weeks," Carl informed them. "She's deserting us for the bush."

"What, leaving you all alone, Carl?" a

young woman asked with a cheeky grin.

"Afraid so," he replied with mock dismay, aware this young woman had been trying all summer long, without success, to match him with Mandy.

"Where are you off to?" someone asked.

"I've taken a week off and I'm going to Whixley. At least, that's where I'll start."

"Where's Whixley?" another asked. "I've never heard of it."

"It's about an hour north of the city, up near Mount Collins," Mandy replied.

"Why would you go there?" the same man asked. "Sounds like it's way out in the sticks and you're a city girl born and bred."

"I'm thinking of living there," she said.

Her colleagues were baffled.

"What about your job?"

"What about us?"

"You'll die of boredom in the bush!"

"I'm not planning to leave my job." Well, not immediately, Mandy thought. "Or my friends," she added.

"With the improved train service Whixley is only about an hour away from the city, so if I moved there it wouldn't take me any longer to commute than it takes some of you to come in from the 'burbs.

"I'd have the best of both worlds."

Her friends weren't convinced.

New Challenges

THE Wednesday before Mandy had phoned the Whixley Commercial Hotel to book a room. She had been looking forward to revisiting the hotel where she'd enjoyed family holidays as a teenager.

"I'm sorry, Mandy, but we're in the midst of modernising so we've nothing available," Brian had told her. "Try the Railway; they've got some nice rooms."

They chatted for a bit about old times.

"Thanks anyway, Brian. I look forward to catching up when I'm in Whixley."

"I'd like that, Mandy."

She drove up to Whixley on Sunday. The temperature was above 40°C as the heat haze danced over the parched country and the road shimmered under the blazing sun.

Mandy blessed her car's air-conditioning.

She arrived in Whixley mid afternoon, checked into the Railway Hotel and rested in her room. The hotel's air-conditioning meant the room was comfortable despite the oppressive heat outside. Thank goodness a cool southerly change was forecast to arrive that evening.

It arrived around six p.m. and the accompanying cool breeze made conditions outside pleasant, tempting Mandy to stroll along the town's single street.

At the far end she discovered a small park beside the Crystal Burn, the creek that trickled behind the main street frontages.

The dappled shade cast by several big, old gum trees presented a calm scene that invited Mandy to sit.

She did so for a time, absorbing the peace and quiet with only bird sounds from the trees overhead and the occasional vehicle passing by. Quite a contrast to the city!

"Beautiful, isn't it?"

Mandy jumped, her reverie broken. She looked up, to see a young woman about her own age. She was a little above average height, with a slim build and short honey-blonde hair framing a friendly smile.

"Sorry to startle you. I'm Emma."

"That's OK, I was miles away. Mandy."

"I haven't seen you around. Are you planning on being here long?"

"It depends," Mandy replied. "I'm thinking of buying a place here."

"You need Larry Lawson. He's the one selling all those hobby farm blocks. But you'll have to wait till he gets back from Melbourne on Tuesday."

Emma told Mandy she was a vet.

"I started up the local practice a couple of years ago. So far it's just me. It can be challenging, but what's life without a few challenges?

"Speaking of Larry, he's OK. In fact I wouldn't have enough business to keep going without all those hobby farmers he's brought here.

"He's a charmer but remember, what Larry does is done for Larry."

With this enigmatic statement Emma ran off in response to a phone call, leaving Mandy curious to meet this Larry Lawson.

On her way back to the hotel she stopped briefly outside the law practice. She recalled Emma's comment and Julian's observations about the challenges involved in running a solo practice.

Maybe a new challenge was what she needed.

* * * *

On Monday morning Mandy woke considerably later than usual, feeling refreshed and relaxed after the best night's sleep she'd had in ages.

She lay for a time, revelling in the knowledge that there were no deadlines to meet; no rush to work. A stark contrast to her hectic Melbourne life!

Eventually she got up and showered before going downstairs to eat a leisurely breakfast while reading the newspapers.

"I could get used to this," she told the waitress who was clearing the table.

"A lot of our city visitors feel that way," the waitress replied.

She confirmed that her boss was due back from Melbourne tomorrow.

"If you want info about the properties he's selling you'll find brochures at reception."

After breakfast Mandy collected several brochures and set off to check out some of the properties listed. She returned hours later, her feeling that Whixley was the place to live reinforced. All that remained was to find a property she could afford.

"Oh, well, no point worrying until I see what's on offer," she told herself while resting on her bed.

An hour later a shower saw her refreshed and ready to meet Brian, who'd invited her for dinner at the Commercial Hotel.

"A chance to catch up on the years since we were kids," he'd said.

Mandy's meal of poached salmon washed down with a nice local wine was excellent.

"I don't think I've had better in Melbourne," she told Brian.

"Our new chef is worth her weight in gold," Brian replied, looking delighted. "We aim to keep the traditional country pub atmosphere but good food is the key to attracting customers, especially these 'tree changers' coming up from the city.

"They expect more than the traditional pub meals of meat and three veg, or fish and chips, though we still do those for our traditional customers.

"It's the same with the rooms. We're installing en-suites because our guests are no longer willing to share bathroom facilities," he added with a chuckle.

The evening passed agreeably as they caught up on the years since they were teenagers. Back then Brian had hardly noticed her, but it was clear he no longer saw her as merely his mates' kid sister.

Mandy enjoyed his company but that teenage crush wasn't rekindled. Or was it?

"You say your family aren't the only Sheltons around here who own a pub?"

"That's right. My cousin, Wilf, has a little pub up in the hills at Shelton's Mill."

"You've even a family town!" She smiled.

"There's not much left since the family's sawmill closed, but Wilf's developed a nice little tourist business to keep the pub open. He's doing quite well."

Brian looked at her.

"I'm going up there on Thursday to see him. Would you like to come along and see some of the mountain country?"

"That sounds lovely. I look forward to it."

The Elusive Larry Lawson

MANDY was waiting for her lunch in the hotel's dining-room on Tuesday when a big, bluff man came up and introduced himself as Larry Lawson, the hotel owner.

In his late thirties, he had an attractive smile. His clothes looked expensive.

"You're the man selling all those subdivision blocks," she replied.

"Guilty as charged." he replied. "I believe you're interested in buying one.

"I'm just back from Melbourne and haven't eaten, so may I join you?"

Over lunch Mandy shared her thoughts about moving to Whixley.

"It's great to see this district going ahead with people like you moving here and bringing new life to the old town." Larry cut a slice from his large steak.

"It's certainly changed from when I came here as a kid with my family," Mandy agreed.

"For the better?"

"Yes, if it means giving people like me a chance to move here and commute to Melbourne."

"This may be your lucky day," he told her. "I have a lovely property that's just become available – ten acres, or, if you prefer, four hectares. It's on Marston Road and if you want to commute to Melbourne it's only ten minutes' drive to the railway station."

Larry went on to extol the property's virtues, explaining it was part of a farm subdivision he was in the process of completing.

Before their meal ended they'd arranged to inspect it together in the morning.

"I'd take you there this afternoon," he apologised, "but I've got an important meeting with the council planning people."

"That's OK, I look forward to tomorrow. I hope you don't have any problems. Some councils can be difficult to deal with."

"Nothing I can't handle. You just have to stay one step ahead of them."

* * * *

After lunch, while Mandy read in a large, cane easy-chair on the hotel's upstairs veranda, Larry was in his office.

With him were Paul Robbins, the bank manager, Frank Barty, the local lawyer and Sean McAlpine, the council's planning officer.

"Thank you all for coming, gents. I'm sure we appreciate that we've done well by helping all those tree changers move here and bring Whixley into this century.

"Of course, it does mean we look after each other."

"Well, we know you've done OK, Larry." Frank poured himself another drink.

"Careful, Frank," Larry warned. "You'd struggle without my business. Don't bite the hand that feeds you."

"Take it easy, Frank. Let's keep it civil," Sean said, trying to keep the peace.

"Thanks, Sean." Larry flashed the planning officer one of his toothy smiles. "Now, what's the latest on those amendments?"

Sean opened his briefcase and pulled out a large file.

"The essence is that a group of farmers are pressing the council to limit any further subdivision of farmland around Whixley. They reckon any more subdivisions will destroy the character of the area.

"Here's the map but remember, this is all confidential until there's a formal proposal for the council to consider. No-one outside my department is supposed to see this yet."

Sean laid out the map.

"As you can see, almost all the land around Whixley that isn't already subdivided will be restricted." He indicated the shaded areas. "The only significant lot not restricted will be Steve Jackson's place, Coolabah Flats, because it's already virtually surrounded by hobby farm subdivisions."

"I made him a generous offer but the drongo knocked me back!" Larry grumbled as he scanned the map.

"I need to develop at least one more property to finance the supermarket and mini shopping-centre I want to build, just out of town on my Marston Road block."

"That's another problem. Some councillors aren't happy about development outside the present town area.

"The extra rates would be welcome but the existing businesses and most of the long-time residents are still living in the past.

"They don't want to see any more change and the councillors are worried about the elections later this year."

"Well, Sean, I pay you to fix these problems so I'm sure you'll find a way around those objections," Larry declared in a tone that didn't invite discussion.

"Paul," he said. "I see Jackson has started building. He must have come into money."

"I approved an overdraft for him. His business case was good so I couldn't see any problem. Sorry, Larry," Paul said.

Larry thought for a minute.

"Maybe it's not a problem. If you called his overdraft in he'd have to sell."

"I can't just call his loan in!" Paul pleaded.

"I only approved it a month ago. I'd have to prove something significant has changed before the regional office would call it in."

"Then something significant will have to be changed," Larry replied.

"That's not so easy," Paul argued. "The Jacksons are one of the bank's oldest customers. If I start upsetting our long-term customers the branch could be in trouble. We're not getting much business from the newcomers . . ."

He trailed off as Larry glared at him.

"That's not my problem! I pay you to fix problems, not to make excuses."

"That's not the only problem with subdividing Coolabah, Larry," Sean added quickly, trying to defuse the situation. "A couple of councillors are talking about placing some sort of Heritage Protection on Coolabah, given its history."

Discussion continued for a while.

"Something's gotta to be done," Larry kept insisting.

Frank had a warning for him.

"Bending a few rules to help a mate is one thing, Lawson, but be very careful before you go any further.

"That can lead to gaol time."

Mandy's Place

NEXT morning Larry joined Mandy at breakfast and shortly after nine drove her out to the Marston Road property, set on a gentle hillside.

Mandy loved it. She was entranced by the view, down over Marston Road and the wide Crystal Burn Valley where extensive flats spread out on each side of the creek.

The flats still seemed to hold a few of the original coolabah trees. When she turned around she was drawn to the blue-green, tree-covered hills that started a little way behind the property and rose back into the Great Dividing Range.

With Larry's help she was soon enthusiastically planning where to build a house and picturing the gardens and orchard she would plant around it.

Then reality hit.

"Larry, it's my dream place and I really want to buy it, but I'll have to check my finances before I can make a commitment."

"Not to worry, Mandy. Let's go back to my office and run through a few figures. We'll see what we can work out.

"I've got a builder I work with and Paul Robbins, the bank manager, is a mate. So I reckon we should be able to swing a good deal for you."

Mandy was elated. Everything seemed to be falling into place.

Even as her lawyer instincts warned her to be careful of any deal that seemed too good to be true, she felt sure it would all check out.

Nevertheless, she'd have an expert property lawyer check the paperwork when she returned to Melbourne.

As they walked back to Larry's car Mandy looked across the valley.

"Who owns the old homestead over there?"

"That's Steve Jackson's place, Coolabah Flats. Though I don't think he'll be there much longer."

"Why's that, Larry?"

"I hear there have been complaints about smells and suchlike from his cattle yards. The bank might be about to start leaning on him – not that I know any details." Larry shook his head.

"That's a shame. Weren't the Jacksons one of the first families to settle in this district?"

"Yep," Larry replied. "But you've gotta move with the times to survive and I don't think Steve Jackson wants to."

He leaned nearer and spoke in a

confidential tone.

"If I can give you a bit of friendly advice, Mandy, don't get mixed up with Jackson. I'd hate to see you get sucked into his problems."

"Thanks for the warning but I think I'll have enough to do getting this house built and moving here without getting mixed up in someone else's problems!"

"That's good." He unlocked his car. "Friends should help each other. And I hope we're friends."

"Of course. And it's really valuable to have someone who knows the area to help me get everything organised and to give me the low down on the locals," Mandy confided as Larry opened the door for her.

Despite her best efforts Larry wouldn't add to what he'd said about Steve Jackson. It made her suspect that there must be something going on between them.

Back at Larry's office, located in one end of the Railway Hotel building, he showed her several house plans before she selected one that appealed to her.

"You've made a great choice. If you position the house right those big windows will give you amazing views over the valley.

"Come to think of it, there's a similar house being built out on York Road. It's just on the other side of the valley from your place. We can run out there after lunch and you can see what you'll be getting."

A warm feeling flowed through Mandy as Larry referred to "your place" – even though she hadn't yet bought it.

"That sounds lovely. I like to see before I commit."

"Good! Let's have some lunch before we go." Larry led the way through a door from his office straight into the dining-room.

After they ate Larry took Mandy out to the partly built house and introduced her to the builder. She was impressed both by the house and the builder who was erecting many of the new homes on the blocks Larry was selling.

"I think we can do you a better deal than the brochure price," the builder told her as Mandy and Larry prepared to leave. "Any friend of Larry is a friend of mine."

Larry took her back to his office where they ran through the figures again and came up with the amount she'd need to borrow.

"Of course you're free to look for finance anywhere, but I reckon you should talk to our local bank manager first. He's a mate and I'm sure he'll look after you.

"You can always check what deals your bank in Melbourne has before you commit yourself," he added.

"Again, thanks for all your help, Larry." Mandy's eyes shone as she considered the possibilities while Larry rang the bank.

"Larry Lawson here. I want an appointment with Paul on Friday morning. It's for a friend of mine. She has to go back to Melbourne on the weekend.

"No, she's not available tomorrow so it has to be Friday.

"I don't care if it is Paul's golf morning; just tell him I said to be available at ten-thirty. OK?

* * * *

While Larry was showing Mandy the block on the other side of the valley, Steve Jackson was on the veranda of the Coolabah Flats homestead.

He savoured the fresh, clean air while looking over the rich creek flats. They were still dotted with the big, old coolabah trees that had given the property its name when his ancestors first settled here 150 years ago.

"Well, Rusty, I don't think I'll ever get tired of this view," he told his Red Heeler cattle dog who sat on the floor beside him.

"And now my overdraft is approved nothing will stop us, eh, old boy?"

A few minutes later a large 4WD ute pulled into the yard. It bore the lettering

"Whixley Fencing & Farm Building Services".

Two men got out. Well-muscled, lean and tanned from their outdoor work, they wore short-sleeved work shirts, shorts and elastic-sided work boots.

"G'day, Don, Rick!" Steve called as Rusty ran to greet them. "Ready to get into it?"

"Sure thing, mate," Don McLeod, the taller of the two, replied as Steve walked over to shake hands.

"We've got those brackets you asked about and I see the other stuff's been delivered."

Rick Southgate, the second man, indicated the pile of timber and steel lying beside a stack of corrugated iron sheets.

"We'll get our gear and make a start," Don announced, heading to the ute. "Power's available on that pole over there, isn't it, Steve?"

Work was quickly underway, with Don and Rick setting out the job on the large concrete slab that had been poured last week while Steve laboured for them.

He was full of confidence for the future, especially now the work had started.

Family History

MANDY woke around six on Thursday morning bubbling with excitement as she thought about spending the day with Brian and seeing the country up in the hills.

Although her teenage crush on him had passed Brian was good looking and very personable, quite a catch for the right girl. And who knew what the future held!

She took a walk before breakfast in the crisp, clean air. When she reached Crystal Burn Park at the end of the street she went over to look at the war memorial.

It featured a WWI Digger wearing a slouch-hat, his head bowed and rifle reversed. He had a bandolier slung across one shoulder and stood atop a simple granite pillar inscribed "Lest we forget".

Below were the names of locals who'd served in the Great War and later conflicts.

Mandy read through the names. Several family names recurred, no doubt the old district families.

One in the WWII list jumped out at her. *Sgt Christopher "Curley" Jackson*.

A star indicated he'd made the supreme sacrifice.

Curley Jackson! Wasn't there a Curley

Jackson pictured with Great-uncle William in her dad's family photo album?

"Goodness, I'd better get moving!" Mandy looked at her watch and hurried back to the hotel to get ready for her trip.

She ate a quick breakfast before dressing with care – casual but smart in a well-cut jacket and trousers, with just a touch of make-up to enhance her natural looks.

Brian arrived promptly at nine.

"Wow, love your car!" Mandy admired the open-top British Racing Green MG-B.

"She's an oldie but a goodie," Brian said proudly as he opened the door for Mandy. "Dad and I are both into restoring old cars. Today is the first time I've taken this beauty out for a longer run.

"I can put the top up if you'd prefer," he added, walking around to the driver's side.

"No, thanks, Brian. It'll be fun driving with the top down. I haven't done that for ages."

As Brian drove out along Marston Road Mandy pointed out the block she was buying.

"I reckon you've got the pick of the blocks along here," he told her, bringing a happy smile to her face.

A little past "Mandy's place" they turned on to the Shelton's Mill road which quickly narrowed as it began climbing into the hills.

There were many sharp bends and side cuttings, with a solid rock wall on one side and a long drop on the other. All demanded concentration.

Watching Brian, Mandy was impressed by his skilled and confident driving.

They stopped at a wayside clearing where an unsealed parking area, composting toilets and two picnic tables with attached seats stood beside a lively creek in the dappled shade of several spreading trees.

"What a delightful place!" Mandy exclaimed as they stood admiring the scene.

"Yes, it's certainly beautiful. Let's have a coffee and a piece of that mud cake Mum packed. Then we can take a walk."

Brian collected the picnic basket from the car and Mandy opened the Thermos and poured coffees while Brian cut the cake.

After returning the picnic basket and securing the car they ambled along the creekside path.

It was very pleasant listening to the bush sounds as they strolled beside the rippling creek, shaded by the overhanging trees.

A hundred metres along Brian pointed to a gully that ran off to the right.

"A couple of kilometres up there you'll find the remains of a dam and a crushing battery. They were built back in the goldrush days, when several small mines operated around here."

"I love hearing about history and the pioneers," Mandy told him.

Brian nodded.

"My ancestors were among the first white settlers in the area and some of them spent time prospecting and mining in these hills before the gold petered out in the 1890s.

"My great-great-grandfather decided he'd make more money running a hotel than mining so he opened the Commercial in the 1880s and we Sheltons have run it ever since."

They returned to the car an hour later and set off to drive the remaining 20 kilometres to Shelton's Mill. As they went further into the hills the road twisted more, with higher drops over the side.

Again Mandy was grateful for Brian's careful skilled driving. She leaned back in her seat and let the fresh wind gently caress her.

"What a perfect day," she said, little foreseeing how it would end.

When they topped the last rise before the road dropped down into Shelton's Mill Brian pulled off the road so they could look down and see the hamlet spread out below.

The half-dozen houses, with the hotel at the top of the street, were scattered over a gently rolling area of about a hectare with a creek flowing off to one side.

"Tourists from Melbourne come up the main road on the other side of the range," Brian explained. "It's much easier than the road we've just taken. That's good for Wilf's business."

For a few minutes they took in the vista then Brian drove down to the Shelton's Mill Hotel where they arrived at lunchtime.

Brian's cousin, Wilf, suggested the ploughman's lunch, a generous meal of bread, cheese, pickles and boiled eggs with sliced ham. While waiting for their meals they took their drinks out to a table on the veranda.

"What a magnificent view!"

Mandy took in the panoramic view of rolling hills covered with blue-green eucalypt bush.

"Thank you for sharing this with me."

"Glad you like it."

Brian cast her a look that seemed to say he no longer regarded her as just his mates' kid sister.

"I don't know what it is, but I'm ravenous." She stretched back in her chair, unsure how she should regard Brian now.

"It's the good mountain air. It gives you an appetite," Brian replied.

They conversed comfortably until their meals came and they ate with relish. The mountain air had indeed given them both good appetites.

After lunch Brian concluded his business with Wilf while Mandy relaxed on the veranda. Then they walked down to explore the old mill site.

"The mill was here and the narrow-gauge railway station just over there." Brian indicated with his hands as he spoke.

"When I was a kid the mill employed around a dozen men and there were another fifteen or twenty cutting and hauling the logs in from the bush.

"By the time it closed there were only three men in the mill and four or five supplying the logs. There were a dozen families here back then; you can see where the houses were on that rise over there."

He pointed behind the mill site.

"The locals always reckoned the pub was built at the top of the street so the drunks only had to roll down the hill to get home!"

"Brian, is that true? Or are you just pulling my leg?" Mandy asked, laughing.

"It's true. At least that's what I was told."

They continued exploring, content and easy in each other's company. At last it was time to go if they were to be back in Whixley before dark.

They walked up to the pub and ordered the coffee-and-cake afternoon tea special.

Again they sat, drinking in the peaceful ambience before they bade farewell to Wilf and set off to drive back to Whixley.

About five kilometres along Brian was carefully rounding a sharp bend when, suddenly, a black 4WD came barrelling around the corner on the wrong side of the road, right in front of them.

The driver was obviously going too fast and taking up the whole road. The vehicle was headed straight for them, almost blocking the narrow road.

Everything seemed to happen in slow motion as Brian tried to control the MG while it moved closer to the edge.

Mandy was flung around by the violent movement until she could see straight down, where a steep slope dropped 15 metres to the creek below. Gravel wreathed in clouds of dust flew over the edge, propelled by the MG's churning wheels.

Mandy shut her eyes and let out an involuntary scream, certain they would plunge down to the creek.

A Narrow Escape

THE two vehicles miraculously passed, allowing Brian to move his car back to the centre of the road. Nothing but a clatter of gravel and dust went over the edge.

Meanwhile the 4WD bounced off the solid rock bank on the other side of the road leaving a scattering of debris as it disappeared around the corner.

When Brian finally stopped the MG in a safe spot Mandy was trembling uncontrollably. She sat, pale and shaking, until he gently helped her out and held her until she was calmer.

Her tears flowed, tears of relief and joy. He continued holding her until they ceased.

"Well, that was a bit scary," Brian said in the typical understated Australian manner.

"Brian, how did you do it? How did you save us?" Her voice wavered as she nestled in his arms.

"To be honest, I didn't have time to think. I just reacted automatically," he replied. "My rally-driving experience was useful. I've been in some tight spots, but never quite that tight.

"I sure hope that's the first and last time!" He helped Mandy back into her seat and leaned on the side of the car, holding her hand. They rested quietly for a few minutes, letting the tension slowly drain away, both very thankful to be unhurt.

"I only hope the next driver he meets is as skilled as you," Mandy said softly.

She looked into Brian's blue eyes and watched the breeze ruffle his hair.

"I'd better go back and see where that drongo hit the bank before we leave," Brian said once he was sure Mandy had recovered.

"I'll check there's nothing on the road that could be a danger to other vehicles. Maybe there will even be something to help identify the idiot."

They walked back together and moved some debris into the roadside gutter where it would be safely out of the way of any passing vehicles.

On their way back to the MG they stopped where a small stream tumbled down the steep hillside before it passed under the road in a culvert.

They took advantage of the ice-cold water to freshen up, washing away signs of their recent ordeal, before resuming their drive.

The remaining trip was uneventful and Brian parked the MG outside the one-officer Whixley police station.

"It's closed!" Mandy exclaimed.

"Not to worry," Brian replied. "A lot of people in the bush who work solo are on call nearly all the time. It makes the job challenging but it also makes it interesting and rewarding."

"Like Emma the vet and Frank Barty the solicitor?"

"That's right. They've got support, but it's usually not immediately right there beside them, so they have to be more self-reliant.

"The payoff is they get to see the real difference they make for real people."

Make a real difference for real people.

Once again those words echoed in Mandy's mind as she wondered about the challenges of running a solo legal practice.

"I'll just report our 4WD friend," Brian said as he walked up the path to the adjoining residence. "I think he might be someone Mick's been after for a while."

Inside the house, Sergeant Mick O'Reilly agreed that Brian's description of the 4WD sounded like one driven by a young fellow he'd been watching out for.

"Thanks for this, Brian. I'll take a run up there in the mornin' and check what's left on the road, then I'll catch up with our young friend.

"Meantime I'll call Wilf up at Shelton's Mill. He might've seen somethin' if the vehicle was headed his way.

"He's not a bad kid but he'll end up killin' himself or someone else unless he smartens up," the sergeant concluded.

"Thanks, Mick." Brian and Mandy turned to leave.

"I don't know about you, but I reckon it's time to eat," he observed as they walked back to his car. "Fancy seeing what our chef has cooked up?"

Soon they were seated in the Commercial Hotel's dining-room, whose door and window-frames were highlighted by elegant, dark-stained trim.

They were served a meal of roast lamb with vegetables followed by pavlova with strawberries and cream for dessert.

"An excellent meal to end an interesting day," Mandy declared with satisfaction.

"I'm pleased you enjoyed it, despite our brush with that 4WD. I hope it won't be the last time we can share a day together." Brian's low, strong voice sent little tingles down Mandy's spine.

They lingered over their coffees until Brian finally walked her across the road to the Railway Hotel.

"Thank you, Brian."

"My pleasure." He hesitated for a long moment, looking into Mandy's eyes.

She was sure he wanted to kiss her but she didn't encourage him and was comfortable when he refrained.

Brian was very good company and she wanted them to remain friends but no more – for now, anyway.

She didn't want the complications of a romance while her house was being built and her move organised. Or was it thoughts of Larry Lawson that held her back?

Driving back to Melbourne on Sunday, Mandy reflected on her week in Whixley.

She had purchased a very desirable block of land, had had a loan approved on favourable terms and had signed to have a house built!

Of course, all these arrangements were subject to the paperwork currently being checked by one of her colleagues who specialised in property law.

In addition, Mandy had met two men, Brian and Larry. Two very different characters, both very attractive.

And what about Steve Jackson? Surely there must be a story there.

Who said the bush was boring?

Girl Next Door

THE following Monday Rick and Don were again at Coolabah, working on Steve's new stockyards.

"So Robbins finally came good with the overdraft!" Don commented as they headed over to the homestead for a mid-morning break. "Didn't you say he was being difficult, Steve?"

"He was, but I think he just likes to prove his own importance. In the end he seemed quite anxious to keep serving some of his 'oldest and dearest customers'," Steve replied, giving a fair imitation of Paul Robbins's ingratiating voice.

"I suppose he has to look after his existing customers if he's to meet his targets," Don mused. "I hear a lot of the newcomers have left their accounts with their city banks, so he's not getting their business."

"Can't say I blame them," Rick put in. "The way he bullies his staff makes it awkward in there at times!"

"I saw that for myself the other day," Steve remarked as they reached the house. "I didn't like it, but you can't chip the bank manager about the way he treats his staff when he's about to approve your overdraft.

"Anyway, on a brighter note you'll find coldies in the fridge over there and I'll grab a tin of bikkies from the kitchen."

They chatted over their ice-cold beers for 10 minutes.

"Just out of curiosity, Steve, has Lawson made an offer for Coolabah?"

"He has and it wasn't half bad. But I told him Coolabah is not for sale, not at any price. The Jacksons have been here for 150 years and I don't want to be the one to end that.

"Anyway, now my overdraft has been approved it's all systems go for my Wagyu beef project."

"We were working for a bloke over near Barton the other day," Rick remarked, reaching for another biscuit. "He thinks he'll make big money out of Wagyu beef.

"You'd better crack on with it, Steve," Don said with a grin. "That other bloke might tie up the market!"

"No worries," Steve replied. "The Japanese market is big and there's growing demand from local restaurants. I reckon there's plenty of room for more producers.

"Even our two local pubs now have Wagyu on the menu."

"And they're charging premium prices," Don put in.

"Yep." Steve smiled. "That means better

prices for me."

"Sounds good, mate." Rick tossed his empty beer can into a nearby rubbish bin. "Farming's been tough with all these dry years."

"You're not wrong there," Steve agreed. "I've got to invest big now but I reckon with a bit of luck I should be pretty well set in a year or two.

"Maybe even be able to move up from the crossbreeds I'm starting with to purebreds. That's where the real money is."

"S'pose you'll be looking to get married, then, mate," Rick said with a cheeky grin at Steve as they stood to return to work.

He winked and gave Don a friendly punch on the arm.

"Better tell your sister to grab Steve before one of these tree changers races him off. I hear Lawson was showing a block on Smethurst's old place to a young woman on Wednesday and she's all signed up.

"That place is just on the other side of the valley and you know what they say about the girl next door!

"Apparently she's quite a looker and a city lawyer to boot. Should have plenty of money," he concluded, grinning.

A bright-blue SUV pulled up and the driver, a tall, vivacious young woman in her late twenties jumped out.

She was dressed in denim jacket and jeans. Fashionable and well suited to her work they also showed her slim figure off to advantage. She wore sturdy but chic work boots and her short, honey-blonde hair framed a confident, friendly smile.

"It's Emma," Don observed. "Hi, sis! What brings you out here?"

"Hi, guys. Thought I'd drop off this drench Steve ordered, seeing I was out this way."

"We were just talking about you," Don said, chuckling, as Emma went to the back of her 4WD to get the drench.

"Yeah, we were just saying you'd better grab Steve before one of these tree changers races him off," Rick said in a playful tone.

"Boys, you all know I'm much too busy for all that romantic stuff," Emma replied with mock seriousness.

She happily entered into the light-hearted banter even as her shining eyes gained added sparkle when she glanced at Steve.

Steve and she had been friends since childhood. Mutual friends often remarked how well matched they were, but so far they appeared to be "just good friends".

Too Good To Be True

BACK in Melbourne Mandy's work colleagues besieged her with questions. She told them about the fabulous block Larry had found for her and the builder who'd build her a house with fantastic views over the valley and surrounding hills.

Her friends rejoiced with her, although Carl offered a warning.

"I don't want to pour cold water on your dreams, Mandy, but be careful that it's not too good to be true."

"Thanks, Carl. Don't worry, I'm getting everything checked by our property section," Mandy assured him.

At lunchtime Mandy and Celia walked to the nearby Flagstaff Gardens to eat lunch.

"So, what's the low-down on Whixley?" Celia asked as they sat in the shade of a Morten Bay fig tree.

"I enjoyed my time there. The more I see of the town and the people, the more I know it's the place for me," Mandy confessed, unwrapping her lunch.

"The people or a particular person?"

"That's a good question," Mandy replied as a warm, pinkish tinge crept up her face.

Celia gave a knowing smile.

"I thought you and Carl might have something going. That's not so?"

"No. Carl's a good friend and I value his advice but he's not my boyfriend." Mandy threw some crumbs to a couple of sparrows that were hopping around nearby.

"I'm glad to hear that. Because, well, I'd like for Carl and me to get friendlier," Celia said shyly. "But I don't want to cut in on you," she added quickly.

"No worries, Celia. I reckon you and Carl are a great match!"

"Thanks, that's terrific. Now, tell me about this particular person in Whixley."

"Actually there are two," Mandy replied with a teasing smile.

"Two? I thought you were looking for a property, not men!"

"Brian runs the Commercial Hotel. Our family stayed there for holidays when I was a teenager. He was my brothers' mate and I had a crush on him."

"An old flame rekindled?" Celia queried.

"No, that's long over, but he's good company. I want to be friends, no more – well, no more at this stage."

Celia gave her friend a long look and raised a questioning eyebrow.

"And the other lucky man?

"Larry Lawson. He's a bit of a hunk and we get on very well. More than that, he's helped me so much.

"He found me this gorgeous block and then organised for his builder mate to build me a great house at a really good price."

"Lucky you got that inheritance last year."

"True, but even then I wondered how I was going to pay for it all until Larry arranged for me to see the local bank manager. That's another story."

"How so?"

"Larry got me an appointment with Paul Robbins, the bank manager, but he wasn't very helpful. 'I have to look after the bank's interests'." Mandy mimicked Paul's pompous condescending tone.

"I don't think he saw a young single woman as a good risk."

"That's a bit archaic!" Celia cried.

"Sure is. I was about to tell him so and leave when Larry came in. Well, you should have seen the change in that pompous, overbearing manager. Suddenly he was falling over himself to help me!

"Apparently the appointment had been made through another staff member and he hadn't realised Larry was involved.

"My loan was approved immediately and at a discounted rate! I could hardly believe it but I've got the paperwork signed to prove I'm not dreaming."

"He sounds too good to be true," Celia

replied slowly.

"I know; fools rush in," Mandy replied. "I'll be careful, but I do have high hopes. Anyway, as I told Carl I'm taking everything to our property section to make sure there aren't any nasties in the fine print."

"That's good, Mandy, I'd hate to see you hurt or worse. Just remember, I'm always here if you need someone to talk to."

"Thanks, Celia. Hey, it's time we were getting back." Mandy stood and brushed a few crumbs off her dark business skirt.

"There's one thing more, but it's strictly confidential," Mandy confided. "Larry introduced me to the local lawyer, Frank Barty. There may be an opening there as he'll probably retire in a year or two."

"Wow, I am surprised! I always thought you were a city girl and your heart was set on climbing the corporate tree here."

"I am, or I was. But people change and I think I'm changing."

* * * *

"Larry? This is a pleasant surprise." Mandy glowed as she took a phone call on the Wednesday after her Whixley visit.

"Yes, I know you said you'd call me when the builder was ready to start, but I didn't expect him to be ready this soon!

"Of course I'm delighted and I don't know

how I'd have managed without your help."

They spoke for several minutes and arranged that Mandy would drive up to Whixley and meet the builder on Saturday.

"Before you go, Larry, our property people checked the paperwork and I'm pleased to say everything's in order.

"Although they did find a couple of things that Frank Barty doesn't appear to have done quite right. Nothing serious and they've sorted it.

"Look forward to seeing you on Saturday. Again, thanks for everything, Larry. Bye."

Mandy sat back in thought. Was it really only a month since she'd started looking for a property in Whixley?

So much had happened so quickly. Larry really did seem to know the right people to get things moving.

She owned a fabulous block and a builder was about to start on her dream house.

In addition, she'd reconnected with her teenage crush, Brian. She suspected he wanted them to be more than just good friends but she was unsure if she wanted that. Time would tell.

Then there was Larry, who set her heart beating faster. Usually warm and helpful, occasionally he showed a ruthless side, especially in business dealings.

Her heart said he was attractive in many

ways but her legal training and instinct advised caution.

There was also Steve Jackson, the subject of Larry's enigmatic warning. There was obviously something between the two men and her curiosity was piqued.

"A penny for your thoughts," Carl quipped, pausing by Mandy's desk

She told him about Larry's phone call.

"This Larry seems to be Mr Fixit," Carl observed. "Maybe more?" He raised one eyebrow.

"I don't know, Carl. Larry has lots of good points, but . . ."

"My advice, for what it's worth, is don't rush into anything. You don't know him properly yet. Play it cool and see what develops over time."

"You're right, of course, Carl. By the way, how is it with you and Celia? I've been so busy I haven't had time to catch up with either of you."

"We're getting on well," Carl replied. "As we get to know each other better we're even surer we'll have a lasting relationship."

"That's fantastic, Carl. I feel you two are meant for each other and I wish you well."

Further conversation was cut short as Morgan Bailey, an older solicitor who supervised induction activities for the new junior solicitors and saw himself as their ongoing boss, came by and frowned at them.

Both Mandy and Carl had moved on from being directly under his daily management but he still retained some authority and for the sake of peace they didn't challenge him.

"Let the old bully have his delusions of grandeur," Carl grinned when Morgan left.

At lunchtime Mandy met Celia in their favourite coffee shop.

"When will you and Carl make the big announcement?" Mandy teased as they ordered fresh fruit smoothies and wraps.

"I know some might say we're rushing things, but I don't think it'll be too long," Celia replied with a dreamy look. "It's not as though we've only just met; we've worked together for ages.

"How about your love life, Mandy?"

"I had a call from Larry this morning," she said, her eyes bright.

She told Celia about the call and about Carl's advice.

"So I've just got to wait and see," she concluded.

Breaking The Rules

LARRY LAWSON was used to getting his own way. Over the past few years he'd done very well from buying up and subdividing broad-acre farmland before selling the blocks to tree changers – people from Melbourne seeking a small rural holding where they could keep a horse or two for the children and possibly also run a few sheep or cattle.

One afternoon in March he summoned Paul Robbins to a meeting in his private lounge upstairs in the Railway Hotel.

"I don't care about your problems, Paul. I want Steve Jackson off that property!"

"Larry, be reasonable. I can't call in his loan without good reason. The Regional Office wouldn't wear it."

Paul clearly wished he was anywhere but in this meeting. A small, sharp-featured man, he was a stark contrast to Larry. He knew his banking career had peaked and now his ambition was to retire in the next few years with a comfortable nest egg.

At first the proposals had seemed simple and safe, bend a few rules, do a few small favours and collect the rewards.

But Larry's proposals had become

relentless demands and the rule-bending became rule-breaking.

"The Regional Office is your problem. I pay you to take care of things."

Seeing Paul's unenthusiastic response Larry leaned closer.

"We wouldn't want anyone to learn about the little deals we've made. Would we?"

"You wouldn't dob me in, Larry?" Paul asked with fear in his voice. "You'd be in trouble, too, if what we've done got out!"

"True, but I'm a land developer. What I've done is just what people expect.

"Sure, I might get some bad press, maybe I might even be fined. But you're a bank manager, a pillar of society and what you've been doing is illegal.

"You could go to gaol. That'd end your career and probably your pension as well."

Paul slumped in his chair.

"I'll see what I can do," he mumbled.

"That's better," Larry told him. "How about another drink before you go?"

"No, I'd better get back to the bank. It's nearly closing time."

After Paul left, heartily wishing he'd never become involved with his schemes, Larry gazed out at Whixley's main street.

He was joined by Frank Barty, an urbane man in his early sixties. He was dressed in a dark business suit which suited the image he tried to create as a respectable lawyer rather than the alcoholic he actually was.

They watched Paul, his head down, cross over to the bank.

"He doesn't look happy," Frank observed.

"I had to lean on him," Larry replied. "I almost feel sorry for him. He was willing enough to take my money; now he has to deliver the goods."

As Larry and Frank watched they saw Steve Jackson come out of the general store next to the bank. He carried a large box which he stowed in the back of his battered old LandCruiser before he drove off.

"Young fool!" Larry exclaimed. "If only he'd accept my offer it'd save us all a lot of trouble. He'd be better off with my money than what he'll get in a forced sale."

"I suppose he can't be blamed for trying to keep the property. After all, it's been in his family for generations," Frank replied.

"True, but there's no room for sentiment in business. If you want to succeed you have to be single-minded.

"One way or another I'll get Steve Jackson out and have Coolabah Flats," Larry concluded grimly.

The Right People

ON Saturday Mandy drove up to Whixley and arrived late morning. She stopped at the Railway Hotel for coffee and cake before driving out to meet the builder.

"Larry's your man to get things done," he told her when Mandy expressed surprise at how quickly the house was progressing.

He was explaining how the house was positioned to take advantage of the views down the valley in one direction and out to the hills in the other when Larry arrived.

"Larry, it's fabulous!" Mandy enthused; her eyes sparkling as she greeted him.

"I reckon we can have it finished in four months," the builder concluded.

"I think this calls for a celebration lunch," Larry said as they walked back to their vehicles. "I'm sure our chef can knock up something special for us."

Back at the Railway Hotel they enjoyed the chef's latest special – spinach salad with warm onions and crispy salami.

"It's a pity you can't stay a bit longer and take advantage of the long weekend," Larry said. "There's a dance tonight that I'd like to take you to."

"I'm sorry, but I promised to be back for

my niece's birthday party tomorrow morning," Mandy replied. "But I'd like to catch up with Emma before I leave."

"I believe she's out of town," he replied and changed the subject.

Back in Melbourne that evening Mandy rang Emma.

"I wanted to catch up while I was in Whixley but Larry said you were out of town."

"I don't know where he got that idea. Sorry to miss you but next time give me a call and we'll make sure we catch up."

Afterwards Mandy couldn't dismiss a nagging little feeling that Larry had deliberately kept her away from Emma. But why would he do that?

* * * *

Over the following weeks Mandy made several trips to Whixley to check on her house. Everything was proceeding smoothly compared with the experience of friends who were building in Melbourne.

While they were frustrated by planning and building red tape, and tradies not turning up when they should, Mandy's house progressed steadily.

It seemed the builder, or more particularly Larry, had an understanding with the local council to minimise red tape and delays.

Thanks to Larry, too, her house had gone straight to the top of the builder's job list.

"You've just gotta know the right people," the builder told her. "Larry sure does – and how to handle them."

In Mandy's experience corporate business often involved personal contacts at the highest levels, so she accepted this.

She found herself attracted to Larry, even if sometimes she felt uneasy about his ruthless approach to business matters.

Brian, by contrast, was a perfect gentleman, well-liked by all.

Although he made efforts to attract Mandy and she really liked him as a friend, her teenage crush wasn't rekindled.

Larry was generally reticent about his personal history although, over lunch one day in mid-May, he told her that he'd left his home in Melbourne's working-class Western Suburbs soon after leaving school.

He'd travelled 4,500 kilometres across the continent to Western Australia's Pilbara Region. There he'd worked in the iron-ore mines for several years.

"It was pretty tough for a young bloke on his own," he admitted. "Most people worked FIFO – Fly In, Fly Out. They'd live in accommodation provided by the mine and work twelve-hour shifts every day for two weeks.

"Then they'd have a week off and fly back to their families in Perth. Some flew to the Eastern States and a couple of blokes even commuted down from Bali.

"I chose to stay on the job during my weeks off and get extra shifts for extra pay."

"That must have made it difficult to see your family," Mandy said sympathetically.

"I didn't see much of them but that didn't worry me. I don't think they missed me."

Mandy, who had always enjoyed close family ties, found this troubling when she mulled it over later.

She guessed he had had to be tough to survive and some of this toughness still showed through. She still felt Larry's good points outweighed his bad.

And what about Brian? It wasn't fair to let him continue hoping they might get together.

One Saturday in June Mandy had dinner with Brian in the Commercial Hotel.

They were both restrained and awkward, almost shy. It was strange, seeing they knew each other so well. A couple of enjoyable meals together had followed their memorable trip to Shelton's Mill.

Now it seemed they both knew what the other needed to talk about but were reluctant to start the conversation.

Instead they filled the silence with inconsequential small talk.

After the waitress had cleared the table and served their coffees Brian's downcast expression told Mandy that he'd guessed what she was about to say.

"I'm sorry, Brian. I know you'd like more than friendship between us, but . . ."

"I understand." His voice was low. "And I respect your feelings. Larry's a lucky man.

"If ever you change your mind, please give me a call," he concluded wistfully.

He walked Mandy back to the Railway Hotel and left her with conflicting thoughts.

Brian was good company, quiet and steady and he headed up the family business. Her mum would certainly consider him a good catch.

But this was her life, not her mother's.

"He's a good friend, but I just don't feel any spark of excitement with him," she told herself. "On the other hand, Larry is entirely different. He certainly provides plenty of spark, possibly a little danger, and he definitely excites me.

"I hope I'm making the right decision," she concluded with a sigh.

Chance Meeting

THE following Monday being the Queen's Birthday holiday Mandy drove up to Whixley on Saturday morning, planning to take advantage of the long weekend.

She would have time to check on her house, which was now at the lock-up stage, and to discuss some fit-out details with the builder.

It would give her time to catch up with Emma and, of course, time to spend with Larry.

When she arrived she expected to meet Larry and the builder. Instead, she found Larry had been unexpectedly called away and had rescheduled the meeting to the afternoon.

This left her at a loose end so she rang Emma.

"Yes, I'd love to catch up for a coffee and chat," Emma said. "How about that new coffee shop opposite the park? Just give me half an hour to finish a couple of things."

"Sounds good," Mandy replied.

"It's great to see you," Emma greeted Mandy when they met in the coffee shop and embraced. "It seems ages since we last got together."

"I know and I apologise," Mandy said as they found a table and sat down. "I keep meaning to meet up with you but every time I'm here there's so much to do with the house."

"And I suppose Larry keeps you pretty busy?" Emma gave Mandy an impish grin.

"We get on very well," Mandy replied primly. "Once I move up here I hope we can build a future together," she concluded enthusiastically.

"I really hope it all works out well for you, Mandy. But, as I've said before, be careful with Larry. I'd hate to see you hurt."

"Larry's a tough businessman but he's been very good to me," Mandy said defensively.

Emma shrugged.

"Don't get me wrong; I'm not against Larry. In fact, I owe him for all the new people and their animals he's brought to the district."

They talked on until their coffee and cake was finished and they strolled over to the park.

There they sat on a bench in the dappled shade and continued chatting until a voice called.

"G'day, Em. Glad I've caught you!"

Mandy turned and saw a well-built man of above average height, whose face was browned from outside work.

He wore an open-necked work shirt, moleskin trousers, elastic-sided work boots and a dark jacket that clearly had seen better days.

He would be handsome if it wasn't for the worry lines creasing his face, Mandy considered.

Somehow his face looked familiar!

"Hello, Steve. What brings you to town?" Emma greeted him.

"I had to pick up a few things and thought I'd check on Rusty while I was in town. Can't run a farm without my cattle dog!"

"You were right, Steve; he'd picked up a bindi-eye. A nasty one, too. It had worked right in between his toes but I got it out and he's OK.

"In fact, you can take him home today, if you like. You'll have to keep an eye on him and make sure he wears a bootie so he can't bite the stitches out."

"That's great, Em! I'll pick him up when you're ready."

As Mandy met the man's gaze she knew who he was instantly. Her breath caught as her heart gave a little flip.

"You're the man I bumped into back in January when my boss and I stopped here for lunch.

"You're Steve Jackson!" she blurted out.

"That's me," Steve replied, allowing a small smile to replace the worry lines on his face.

Again that spark jumped between them.

Mandy pushed it aside, believing Emma was Steve's girlfriend. Anyway, she wasn't interested in a boyfriend at present.

She remembered Larry's warning.

"And particularly not a boyfriend with problems," she told herself firmly.

Organising the house and the move to Whixley were providing enough challenges to keep her busy.

Besides, if she were to be in the market for a boyfriend it would be Larry, wouldn't it?

"You two are neighbours, you know," Emma declared, smiling broadly at them both. "We'll have to organise a welcome party when you move here Mandy."

Later when she met Larry, for some reason Mandy didn't tell him she'd been speaking to Emma and Steve Jackson.

Moving Day

TO Mandy's delight the builder was as good as his word and completed her house in four months. She took a month's leave to move and settle into her new home.

The only downside was moving in July, the middle of a particularly wet winter.

She arrived in Whixley one Saturday morning and soon afterwards ran out to greet Celia and Carl who'd driven up to see her new home and help her move in.

The rain that had been falling constantly for a week now stopped, allowing the pale winter sun to show the valley and surrounding hills in all their glory.

"Wow, Mandy, it's beautiful!" Celia enthused, admiring the view from Mandy's front veranda. "That roadside wattle is magnificent," she added, indicating the trees covered in tiny yellow blossom balls.

"I just know coming here is the right move," Mandy answered. "Maybe we'll see you and Carl move up here!"

"Hmm, I think we might just limit ourselves to visiting," Carl said, joining them. "I don't think we're ready for a tree change. Not yet, anyway."

"Who's for coffee?" Mandy asked. "I've a

picnic basket so we can have it here on the veranda before the removal guys arrive."

"Coffee and cake? You'd hardly know we're in the bush!" Carl, always the joker, quipped as Mandy placed a tray on the picnic table he'd set up.

"I know land and houses are cheaper in the country but how could you afford all this on one income?" Celia asked, sweeping her arms around.

"Carl and I fear that, even with two incomes, it'll be years before we can buy a home. And then we'll only be able to afford a small apartment."

"You're right, I couldn't afford to buy in the city. My inheritance helped but I still needed the loan Larry organised."

"Good old Larry," Carl teased. "When do we get to meet him?"

"Hopefully at lunchtime," Mandy replied, her face glowing and eyes sparkling. "But right now we've work to do," she added as the removal van arrived.

The driver and his assistant quickly unloaded Mandy's possessions, then she and her friends began organising the house.

"You'll need more furniture," Celia said as they arranged Mandy's lounge. "It's much roomier than your old apartment."

"Yes, it's wonderful, but I won't rush into buying things. I want to take my time and make it perfect."

Around 12.30 Mandy stretched.

"Let's go into Whixley and grab some lunch. The Railway puts on good meals."

They cleaned up and half an hour later were ordering drinks and meals when Larry came into the hotel. He greeted Mandy with a quick embrace.

"Larry, these are my friends, Celia and Carl. They're helping me move in."

"I guess we can call you a local now, Mandy." Larry gave her a warm smile.

She invited Larry to join them and soon they were enjoying their meals. Celia and Carl started some light-hearted teasing about how well Mandy and Larry got on.

Mandy denied any special interest in Larry, apart from him being a good friend who'd been so helpful during her move.

The growing pink spots on her cheeks and the sparkle in her eyes undermined her protests, however.

Larry insisted the meals and drinks were on the house as his welcome present for Mandy and her friends.

"Larry's quite a man," Celia commented as they drove back to Mandy's house. "I don't want to be negative but don't you think he's almost too good to be true?"

"I know what you mean, Celia, but Larry's OK. Sure, he's a hardnosed businessman, but I suppose he has had to be to get where he is."

"All I'm saying is be careful, Mandy."

That night, in bed, Mandy could hardly believe her dream had come true so quickly. She was lying in her own new house in an idyllic setting!

She marvelled at how well everything had worked out and again appreciated Larry's big and helpful part in it all.

Were their futures tied together? The more she thought about this the more appealing it became.

True, Larry wasn't exactly a film-star type; rugged was the better word to describe him.

But he was established and well off, plus he'd been most generous with his time and help ever since their first meeting.

Above all, they got on well and there was certainly more than a frisson between them.

A future shared with Larry Lawson sounded most attractive. So why did these niggling little doubts persist?

They were probably just nerves, Mandy concluded, and pushed them aside before falling asleep.

Complaints

ACROSS the valley Steve Jackson, Rick Southgate and Don McLeod were finishing off Steve's new stockyards.

"Ah, life's good." Don paused for a moment to contemplate the sunlit vista.

"You're not wrong there, mate," Rick agreed. "Maybe now we can catch up on those jobs we've had to put on hold with all that rain.

"The rain's been good but I reckon we've had enough of a good thing for a while," Steve said, joining Don and Rick to admire the view.

"This is a beautiful place and that's only one reason why I'll do all I can to keep it," he declared.

Don, who was very perceptive, picked up on Steve's comment.

"You sound like there's something wrong, mate. What could stop you keeping Coolabah?

"You're set now you've got your overdraft and it looks like being a good season."

"I wish it was that simple, Don."

Steve sighed and leaned against the stockyard fence.

"Paul Robbins called me into the bank the other day. Said there'd been complaints about smells and noise from my place.

"He advised me to accept Lawson's offer to buy Coolabah. He said that would be a lot easier for everybody.

"When I asked what he meant by 'easier for everybody' he just mumbled something about looking having to look after the bank's interests."

"He's a nasty piece of work," Rick commented.

"But that's not all," Steve continued. "I had a call from Sean McAlpine, the council planning bloke. Would you believe he wants to review my planning permit because he's also had complaints?

"He also said it would be easier for everyone if I accepted Lawson's offer."

"He was that blatant?" Rick asked.

"Yeah," Steve answered. "I reckon he thinks Lawson will protect him."

"Gee, that's tough," Don commiserated. Can't you fight them somehow?"

"I dunno," Steve replied. "Banks and councils, they seem to make the rules to suit themselves.

"And the problem is I don't have the money to take them on."

"I've reckoned for a while there's dirty work afoot with Lawson and that bank manager," Rick said, disgusted. "And now it seems the council planning bloke is involved, too."

"Ironic, isn't it? Just when everything is looking up this happens," Steve said despairingly. "It's a real kick in the guts."

The three men continued to discuss the injustice of it all intermittently while they worked, but they failed to come up with any answers.

Don changed the subject.

"Hey, Steve, your new neighbour over the creek is moving in."

They looked across the broad valley to where a furniture van and two cars were parked beside the house that had been built during the last few months.

Several people were taking things from the vehicles into the house.

"Is she the one you reckon has been complaining?" Don asked.

"I wish I knew," Steve replied. "But it's a bit coincidental how these complaints only started after that woman and her city cronies started coming up here."

He pushed back his hat and scratched his head.

"I'm not against tree changers but I really think, if these people are gonna move to the country, they have to accept that it's a farming area and that means farm noises and smells!"

Further speculation about tree changers and complaints was interrupted by the arrival of a small SUV.

"It's Emma," Don observed. "Hi, sis! What brings you out here?"

"I've come to check on Steve's cow," Emma replied, walking towards the back of her vehicle to fetch her overalls and equipment.

"Thanks for coming out at such short notice," Steve said. "Do you want a drink before you start?"

"No, thanks. I had one just before I left." She flashed Steve a smile. "Besides, I'd better keep moving. I've got a busy day ahead."

Steve and Emma went to check on the cow that was lying with her newborn calf on a bed of hay in a corner of the partly built stockyards.

Emma quickly determined that the cow had milk fever.

"This calcium shot should fix her. Then keep an eye on her and call me if she's no better," she instructed.

As they walked back to her vehicle Emma moved closer to Steve.

"Will we see you at the dance on Saturday night?"

"I dunno, Em. With all that's going on I

can't raise much enthusiasm for socialising right now."

"Come on, Steve, that's just why you need to get out and take your mind off your problems," she replied, putting a friendly arm around his shoulders.

Back at the vehicle Emma removed her overalls and prepared to leave.

"Saturday night, then?" She looked directly at Steve with another brilliant smile.

"How can a man resist that smile? Yes, Em, I'll be there on Saturday.

"Scout's honour," he added when she gave him a disbelieving look.

As Emma drove off Steve rejoined Don and Rick.

"I think my sister's got a thing for you," Don said, winking at Steve.

"I like her and I really admire the way she's set up her practice; we've needed a vet for a long time. But I can't make any commitments with all this hanging over me and Coolabah," he replied.

Around eleven, with the job finished, they all went home to clean up before meeting in Whixley for lunch.

"After that we can go to the footy. The Bulldogs are playing at home this week and if they win they're in the four!" Rick said, picking up his tools and heading for his vehicle.

By 12.30 they were seated by a front window in the Commercial Hotel dining-room with large plates of steak, chips and vegetables beside their pots of beer.

Like most of the longer-established residents they preferred the Commercial's old-style country pub atmosphere, whereas Larry had moved the Railway Hotel upmarket since he had acquired it two years ago.

This meant it was now the pub of choice for many new arrivals and most young people.

"Look, Steve! Isn't that your neighbour over there with Lawson?"

Don gestured as they were finishing their meal.

The three men looked across the road and spotted Mandy and Larry emerging from the Railway Hotel along with another couple.

Mandy and Larry embraced before he drove away, leaving Mandy, Celia and Carl to stroll along the street.

A Warning

AFTER Celia and Carl returned to Melbourne Mandy went into Whixley to meet Larry for lunch at the Railway Hotel.

"We'll be able to see a lot more of each other now you're a local," Larry said as they settled in his private lounge. "I've been saving this wine for a special occasion."

Over a leisurely meal they continued exchanging their life stories. Larry, who'd previously revealed little of his personal history, now opened up.

"If you want success you have to take risks, climb out of your comfort zone.

"Look at me. I'm the oldest of a large family. My parents didn't have much so I left school as soon as I was old enough."

"That must have been hard." Mandy valued education.

Larry shrugged his shoulders and grinned.

"I wasn't that keen on school. So, as I told you the other day, I went to the West and got work in the mines.

"It was hard but the pay was good, especially for a young fella with no qualifications or experience.

"A lot of the blokes drank and played hard. They lost most of their pay quickly."

"Not you?"

"No way! I couldn't see any sense in working just to give someone else my hard-earned money. I saved every cent I could, then started investing in property."

"It must have taken a lot of self-control to keep away from all that drinking and gambling," she commented.

"It sure did. But you should know by now that when I set a goal nothing stops me reaching it.

"After a few years I came back to Victoria and got a job in real estate. I wanted to learn the game so I could do my own deals without paying an agent. More importantly, I wanted to make sure I got the best deals.

"While I was working with the estate agent I saw there was big money to be made buying farmland to subdivide and then selling the blocks to tree changers."

"Like me?" Mandy chuckled.

"Well, not all the deals were like yours – a special deal for a very special person."

With that he reached across the table and placed his hand over Mandy's.

Mandy had told Larry how she'd grown up in Melbourne's leafy Eastern Suburbs.

"Your background's a bit different from mine," he said with no trace of rancour.

"Well, my parents supported me through school and university and till I got my job as junior solicitor in a big law firm. I guess I never had to struggle like you.

"Most people think it's a dream job but I'm tired of all the big city rush. The laidback pace here suits me much better."

"I know what you mean," he replied. "Whixley is close enough to the city for us to enjoy the benefits but far enough away that we don't have the hassles!"

The waitress arrived with their desserts, crème brulée for Mandy and a sticky date pudding for Larry.

"I think you'd do well in your own law practice, Mandy. Maybe you could take over here in Whixley when Frank retires.

"He's no spring chicken and he's not in good health," he added thoughtfully.

"I like that idea but, of course, it all depends on Frank retiring and how much he'd want for his practice.

"I'd need to get experience in running a solo practice, too."

"Maybe that can happen," Larry replied. "Why don't I arrange for you to spend a few days with Frank next week so you can get the feel of a small practice?"

"That would be fabulous, Larry! But are you sure it'll be OK with Frank? I don't want to be a nuisance."

"Of course. Frank always has more work than he can handle – he'll appreciate some help. Besides, he owes me."

The following week Mandy spent some days with Frank, who had been a very competent and successful general solicitor before drink caused his standards to slip.

He gave her a lot of valuable tips about running a small practice.

"I've thoroughly enjoyed the challenge and I've learned so much about running a solo practice!" Mandy told him on their final day together. "Thank you very much for your time."

"My pleasure," Frank replied in his courteous manner. "I think you'll do very well in a solo practice. You learn quickly and aren't afraid to ask questions.

"One final thing," he added as Mandy was leaving. "Be careful of Larry Lawson. Don't let him get you in his clutches and destroy you . . . like he's destroying me."

The last words were barely audible, leaving her unsure if she'd heard correctly.

She found it hard to believe Larry posed any danger to her. After all, he was so helpful and they seemed to be well suited romantically.

Nevertheless, she vowed, she'd keep her eyes open.

Stranded!

BY mid-August Mandy was settled in her new home and was due back at work in Melbourne in another week.

She went into Whixley to meet Larry and they sat by the fire in his private lounge. The rain, which had stopped briefly, had returned and beat down outside.

She was almost asleep, wrapped in a warm glow that wasn't all due to the fire.

Suddenly Larry's phone rang, startling her awake as he stood to answer it.

"Paul!" Larry snapped.

He listened for a minute then his voice became hard and demanding.

"What do you mean, all you can do is send Jackson a threatening letter? Don't give me that rubbish!"

Mandy was shocked to see how cold and hard his friendly face turned as he spoke.

"Just get it done. No excuses."

He terminated the call and turned back to Mandy, his face relaxing.

"Sorry about that. Seems if I want anything done properly I have to do it myself."

"I hope there's nothing wrong."

"Nothing serious, just a bit annoying. I'm

sorry, Mandy, I have to attend to some business. Thanks for a nice afternoon; I hope it won't be our last."

"I hope to spend more time with you. Have you thought any more about that show in Melbourne next Friday?"

"Yes, and I'd really like to go with you. Can I give you a ring tomorrow? I'll have a better idea of what I'm doing next week after this meeting I'm off to now."

They parted, Larry to his meeting and Mandy to drive home. This time, when they embraced before parting, Mandy didn't hold back as she'd tended to do previously.

This time led to a long, satisfying kiss that left Mandy tingling all over. All thoughts of Larry's reaction to the phone call slipped from her mind.

When she got outside she found the rain had stopped again so she decided to explore the district rather than drive directly home.

Two hours later she was driving along York Road over the valley opposite her place. At the top of a long steady rise she pulled over and stopped to look across the valley towards her home.

The picture made by the sun setting over the mist shrouded hills behind her house was delightful.

She leaned against the car savouring the

memory of Larry's kiss while basking in the peaceful beauty before her.

"I'm so glad I moved to Whixley," she said aloud.

Was it to convince herself her new home, Whixley and her growing relationship with Larry were real and not just a fantastic dream that would vanish when she woke up?

A little after the sun slipped behind the hills she became aware that the air was nippy and her light jacket was no defence against the growing chilly wind.

"Time to get going," she muttered and slowly turned from the fading scene.

To her dismay, when she attempted to drive off the car's wheels started spinning on the wet grass.

Being a city driver with little experience on unsealed surfaces, she made the mistake of revving the engine which caused the wheels to spin even faster and sink into the sodden ground.

"Oh, no!" she exclaimed in frustration.

She guessed she would have to call the RACV to tow her out. It was a good thing, she reflected, that her parents had signed her up for emergency roadside assistance.

She pulled her phone out and cried out again in dismay. What a time for her phone to die!

The peace and joy that had so recently washed over her evaporated and was replaced by concern.

She was stuck out here alone with darkness quickly approaching. The irony was that she could actually see her own house on the other side of the valley, no more than 20 minutes' walk away if there were a path straight across.

But there was no path and the Crystal Burn creek that normally meandered quietly through the valley was now running high and fast. There was no way across.

In addition Mandy's shoes, fashionable and quite adequate for town walking, were totally unsuitable for walking in this saturated landscape.

For several minutes she sat there, half listening while the radio played in the background and the rain, which had started again, drummed on her car.

In vain she tried to remain calm and think about what to do.

No answer came.

She was stuck. She would just have to spend the night in the car and hope for someone to come along and help her in the morning.

Suddenly the voice on the radio grabbed her attention.

"Just repeating that police warning. Earlier

today two violent prisoners escaped from the Mount Collins Correctional Centre.

"They were last seen late this afternoon in the Whixley area where they broke into a house and stole clothing including raincoats and hats.

"Do not approach these men under any circumstances.

"Anyone with information should immediately call Crime Stoppers on 1800 333-000. Now it's on with the music!"

Mandy peered into the gathering gloom and rain, grateful that the car would at least keep her dry.

Still, she faced a cold night with only her thin jacket for a covering.

Suddenly her heart was pounding and her hands clenched the steering wheel. Who, or what, was that dark shadowy form coming out of the gloom towards her?

The next moment a man knocked on her car window and called for her to open the door.

He was wearing a long raincoat and his face was almost hidden by his pulled-up collar and pulled-down hat.

An Old Photograph

STEVE JACKSON was driving through the downpour when he noticed a parked car. With no-one around and no houses nearby he stopped to investigate.

He donned his oilskin coat, pulled his hat down against the rain and walked over to the car.

However, when he tapped on the window the driver ignored him, resolutely staring straight ahead.

"Mandy!" he called. "It's me, Steve."

But she didn't respond.

"Mandy, open the window!"

Finally she recognised his voice.

"Steve, is that you?" Her voice trembled.

"Sure is. Are you OK? What are you doing out here this late and in this weather?"

"I stopped to watch the sunset and my car got bogged and my phone died!" The words rushed out, falling over each other.

Steve spoke gently while she calmed down and the rain eased to a light drizzle.

Eventually she climbed out. He held his coat open to shelter her from the cold wind while she leaned against him, drawing support and comfort.

Once she regained her composure Steve

studied her.

"Are you ready for us to tow your car out of here now?"

"I think so," she replied in a small voice.

"OK, I'll get my LandCruiser hooked up."

He connected a tow-rope and pulled Mandy's car on to the road. But when she tried to start it the engine wouldn't fire up and meanwhile the rain intensified.

"We can't do much in all this rain," Steve advised. "We'll have to leave it here and come back in the morning."

"What will I do?" Mandy wailed. "I can't walk home in this weather!"

"No worries, I'll drive you," he replied in his easygoing manner.

"I can't put you to all that trouble."

"No trouble. Ten minutes into town and another ten out to your place. We'll push your car off the road and you can pick it up in the morning."

They were on their way to town when they met with a torrent of water as the normally placid Crystal Burn now swirled over the bridge near Whixley.

"This isn't good," Steve said. "The creek can come up like this after heavy rain in the hills but it's a while since I've seen it this high. It's too dangerous to cross in the dark.

"We'll have to go back to Coolabah and hope it's gone down by morning."

Fifteen minutes later Steve was stoking the open fire in Coolabah's lounge. In the kitchen the kettle was boiling and frozen meals were heating in the microwave.

At first conversation was tentative, but Steve's open manner and Mandy's natural friendliness soon dissolved the barriers and they began swapping life stories.

Mandy explained how she'd become disenchanted with city life and wanted a more relaxed lifestyle while keeping her city-based job. At least for now.

"So, that's my story, what about you?" She settled back in the comfortable armchair, more at ease than she'd have expected to be when alone with the enigmatic Steve Jackson.

"My ancestor, Richard Jackson, came out from Yorkshire in the 1860s to seek his fortune on the goldfields.

"Like most Diggers he didn't make his fortune, but he fell in love with this new land, so different from the Old Country.

"He bought land at the Crown Land Sales; a whole square mile of it. This was far more than the younger son of a yeoman farmer could ever dream of owning in England.

"It only cost him one pound an acre and he could pay it off over time. He risked everything to raise the deposit on the land and to buy stock.

"Half his land was on the prime flats and rising country along the valley between you and me. That rich soil was the foundation of Coolabah's prosperity. The other half ran back into the foothills of the Great Dividing Range.

"True, it required hard work to bring the land into production. And the Jacksons have been working since then to keep Coolabah, through good times and bad."

"Coolabah sounds pretty special. Tell me, where did the name come from?"

"Originally there were big coolabah trees scattered all over the creek flats. The open country between them was a real bonus because Richard could graze his cattle without first clearing the land."

Just then the microwave pinged and Steve fetched their meals.

Mandy pulled up two side tables so they could eat by the fire.

"I didn't realise I was so hungry," she confessed.

"It's the country air." Steve smiled as he sat down and they began to eat.

"So Christopher Jackson, listed on the war memorial, is one of your relations?" she asked after a while.

Steve collected their now empty plates.

"Yeah. He was my grandfather's older brother. He was in the Militia, the part-time

Army Reserve, and was sent to New Guinea when the Japanese invaded in 1942.

"Some people called them 'Chocos' – Chocolate Soldiers who would melt in the heat. They said the only real soldiers were the AIF, the full-time Australian army who were fighting over in North Africa.

"But they were wrong. Those Chocos soon proved they were as good as any soldiers. A lot didn't return."

"Christopher?" Mandy asked quietly.

"He and many others."

"That's so sad, all those young lives lost. My grandfather's older brother was lost up there, too. I wonder if they ever met."

She recalled the picture of Bluey and Curley in her father's photo album.

"Hang on, I've a picture of him somewhere."

Steve left and returned with an old album which he placed on the coffee table and turned over several pages.

"Ah, here he is."

Mandy's heart jumped as she saw the picture of two young WW2 soldiers.

"But, but that's my great-uncle, Bluey Cameron, with him!".

"What do you mean?" Steve asked, baffled.

"My dad has this exact same picture in his family album!"

Mandy's voice had risen with excitement.

"And Bluey didn't come back from the war, either."

"Well, it sure is a small world," Steve said. "Life's full of little surprises. Fancy you and me having this in common!"

The microwave pinged to say their dessert was ready.

"Will you have ice-cream or custard with your apple strudel?" he asked.

"Can I be naughty and have both?" Mandy cast him a mischievous look.

"And cream?" Steve responded, going to fetch their desserts.

"Yes, please!" she replied, going with him to make another pot of tea.

Soon their empty plates were stacked in the dishwasher while they relaxed again by the fire.

"Emma tells me my place used to be part of Coolabah," she remarked.

"That's right," Steve answered. "My great-grandmother had to sell a hundred acres across the creek when Christopher fell in New Guinea and her husband died soon afterwards.

"The bank wouldn't extend her overdraft. Apparently a widow and her sixteen- year-old son weren't considered an acceptable risk, even though she was an experienced farm manager."

"That's so unfair!" Mandy said.

"Well, that's the way banks were, and still are, as far as I can see."

His voice was tinged with bitterness.

"Most farmers need bank finance but the banks only provide credit while it suits them. Woe betide the farmer when it no longer suits their bank to provide funds," he added flatly.

"My bank manager is my main problem right now. Paul Robbins is about to cut off my credit.

"He's putting the blame on complaints to the council about my place, even though I've assured him any problems have been fixed.

"He told me he thought my Wagyu beef business case was sound but all of a sudden he's changed his mind and is about to call in my overdraft and force me off Coolabah!"

He stopped and shook his head, bemused. He hadn't meant to tell Mandy his troubles, but the words just flowed out naturally in the cosy, relaxed setting.

"That's terrible!" Mandy exclaimed with sympathy he could tell was genuine. "Isn't there anything you can do?"

"If only I knew who was complaining I'd talk to them, show them how I've fixed the problems. But the complaints are anonymous, or the council just won't say who it is.

"My guess is it's some of these tree changers. You would think they'd have the guts to speak to me first," he answered, his anger evident.

"I'm a tree changer, Steve, but I hope you don't think I'd stoop so low," Mandy answered with conviction and a steady gaze towards Steve.

Although at one point he had wondered, one look into her eyes convinced Steve she was telling the truth.

"No, I don't believe you'd be so low. But Larry Lawson is another matter."

"What do you mean?"

"I'm sorry, Mandy, I know you and he are friendly. I simply don't trust him. He's tried very hard to buy Coolabah for his development company.

"He wasn't happy when I refused to sell. Now the bank and the council are both leaning on me to sell to him."

"I'm sure you're wrong, Steve. I know Larry can be a hard businessman but he's been very helpful to me and I've never had reason to doubt his honesty."

"Maybe you're right. Maybe I'm just paranoid." Steve sighed.

As they stared at each other a spark jumped between them and Mandy again felt that frisson of excitement she'd felt when they'd bumped into each other back in January.

She tried to rationalise it away, to ignore it. She was interested in Larry, wasn't she?

And he had warned her about Steve Jackson.

But all her intentions were undermined when, without meaning to, she began comparing genuine, open, friendly Steve with Larry.

Usually a charmer, and one who'd certainly been helpful, Larry also had a cold, hard and even ruthless side.

Had Mandy but known, at the same time Steve was finding himself drawn to Mandy, but two things stood in the way of any deeper relationship.

Wasn't she Larry's girlfriend? And, besides, right now the battle to save Coolabah required his full attention.

So the moment passed, even though he was becoming more and more convinced that a girl like Mandy was wasted on a bloke like Larry Lawson.

Steve dragged his eyes away from Mandy to check the large mantelpiece clock.

"Crikey, look at the time! Do you want another cuppa before we turn in?"

"No, thanks, I'll just hit the hay. It's been a big day."

"You'll find towels and all in the en-suite."

Steve showed Mandy to a guest bedroom and gave her a big T-shirt to sleep in.

"Just help yourself to what you need and I'll see you in the morning."

Mandy turned on the electric blanket, showered and was soon snuggled down in bed. The rain drummed on the galvanised iron roof and the wind gusted around the solid old house.

As she drifted towards sleep her thoughts drifted back over their conversation. Surely Steve was wrong to think Larry would stoop to dirty tricks.

Next morning the creek was down so they towed Mandy's car to the Whixley garage. Steve was about to take Mandy home when Larry came to collect his car which was in for a service.

He wasn't happy to see Mandy with Steve but her quick explanation calmed him before they left together.

Mandy saw the tension between the two men and wished they could be friends.

Unfair Accusations

ONE Friday in mid-September Mandy returned from Melbourne earlier than usual. Larry saw her stop briefly in town and thought she looked upset, but he was busy.

"I'll catch up with her tomorrow," he told Frank as they went to his office.

He didn't see Mandy get home and fling herself on her bed, sobbing.

"It's so unfair, but what can I do? I could lose everything!"

Next morning she woke early to a beautiful spring day. The sun beamed down from a clear blue sky where a few wispy clouds floated on the gentle breeze.

Two magpies carolling outside her window and a kookaburra laughing from the tall gum tree helped her temporarily to forget her problems.

Then yesterday's events flooded back, threatening to fill her with despair .

"Wallowing in self-pity won't get you anywhere," she chided herself.

She dressed and had a quick breakfast before going to work in her garden to try to dim her worry and feelings that she'd been treated so unfairly.

She reflected how quickly life could

change. How her career, so settled seemingly, had ended.

By ten o'clock she'd worked the edge off her concerns and was heading inside for a cuppa when Larry's car pulled up.

"Have you forgotten our date?" he asked, gesturing to her gardening clothes.

Then she remembered their plan to drive up to the picturesque little pub in the hills, the one she'd gone to with Brian.

Things had changed since then.

"No, I . . ." She started to cry.

"Mandy, what's wrong?" he asked with genuine concern. He took her in his arms.

"It's so unfair!" she sobbed.

"Shh. Calm down and tell me your problem. Then we'll fix it," Larry said gently but firmly. "Most things can be fixed one way or another."

Mandy turned her tear-stained face to him and poured out her story.

How her employment had been abruptly terminated yesterday when Morgan Bailey, the office bully, accused her of stealing from the petty cash.

"I'd never steal! Apart from anything else it only holds $300. As if I'd risk my career for that!" she finished.

"What a rat! Can't you appeal?"

"Morgan Bailey is a nasty, cunning old man," Mandy replied. "He knew that Celia,

Carl and the boss were at a conference in Las Vegas. Most of the other staff were also away, leaving him in charge.

"He told me to go quietly and no more would be said. Otherwise he'd have me charged which could finish my career.

"I was shocked and couldn't think straight so I, well, I just signed the resignation letter he prepared and left," Mandy concluded.

Larry, always ready to take advantage of any situation, thought quickly.

"I think I've an answer that will help us both. Frank Barty is getting on. I'm sure he'd welcome a bright young assistant and you've already worked with him.

"Besides, he owes me. I'll have a word."

"Oh, thank you, darling Larry!" Mandy exclaimed, embracing him. "What would I do without you? You're a real friend."

"What are friends for if they can't help you?" Larry smiled, pleased with the turn of events.

"Now, while you change I'll see what I can find in your pantry for us to have with a coffee before we go."

Larry acted quickly on his idea and an excited Mandy started work with Frank the following Monday.

If everything worked out as expected she'd have an opportunity to take over the business when Frank retired in a year or two. Meantime she'd gain valuable experience in a small legal practice.

Her disappointment and fear for her future was replaced with joyful anticipation.

Again Larry's help had been invaluable, but was that enough to build a lasting relationship?

She was becoming surer that it was.

* * * *

A few days later she was woken by her phone ringing.

"You've what?" she asked after a short conversation. "Slow down, Celia, it's five a.m. here and I'm only half awake!

"I thought you said you're getting married today! Aren't you and Carl in Las Vegas for a conference?"

"It started as a joke," Celia explained. "You know what a joker Carl is. But then we decided, why not? It was an opportunity to do something really different. And we both want a small wedding with no fuss."

"Wow! I hardly know what to say, except congratulations and best wishes!" Mandy was still trying to take in the news.

"Gotta go, Carl says the limo is waiting," Celia said. "I'll send you some pics!"

Mandy lay back on her bed.

"Well, I'm not the only one to spring a surprise," she decided. "But Celia's surprise beats mine!"

That afternoon Mandy received an e-mail and the promised photos. Celia looked radiant in a white linen pants suit while Carl was his usual dapper self in a dark tuxedo.

Celia was clearly thrilled.

Our hotel is right on the Strip and you wouldn't believe the size of our room.

The bathroom area alone is bigger than most hotel rooms in Melbourne; it even has two hand-basins and two loos. There's a big bath and a huge shower.

We've seen several shows by well-known artists and the costs are minimal. The whole economy is based on gambling.

The Strip is lined with casinos, all featuring different themes, and we even saw pokies, (they call them slot-machines here) as soon as we entered the airport terminal!

Celia continued in a happy, very upbeat tone as she told Mandy about their trip out to the Grand Canyon.

Some people might say we're rushing into marriage, she concluded her e-mail, *but we've worked together for ages and we're both sure we've made the right decision.*

Mandy was very happy for her friends, but couldn't help wishing her love life was as straightforward as theirs.

The Vet Calls

A WEEK later Steve was checking his stock one stormy evening. Although spring had started three weeks ago winter was having one last fling.

"Oh, no!" he exclaimed as he saw the shed door swinging in the wind.

That door should have been securely closed to keep his prize cow, who was about to calve, safe and out of the weather.

Steve hurried over, to have his fears confirmed; the cow was gone. After a short search he found her out in the paddock inadequately sheltered under a small tree.

His experienced eye immediately saw she'd started to give birth but something was wrong.

"Don't worry, old girl, we'll soon get you some help."

Steve pushed through the storm back to the house and phoned Emma.

"I hate to ask you to come out in this weather but I can't afford to lose her, or the calf."

"Of course I'll come. See you shortly."

"Thanks, Em, you're a treasure."

True to her word, Emma was soon there and half an hour later a healthy bull calf was delivered.

Steve fetched his LandCruiser, placed the calf in the back and drove over to the shed, the cow following behind calling to her calf.

Soon both were comfortably settled in the shed with the door secured.

"We're a handsome couple," Emma said, casting Steve a lively smile. "Just look at us, soaked to the skin and covered in mud!"

"Do you want to come over to the house and clean up?" Steve asked.

"That would be great. Luckily I always carry a change of clothes for these jobs. I'll get my things from the SUV."

"I'll put the kettle on."

In the house Steve showed her to a shower while he went to another. Soon they were clean, warm and resting in front of the blazing fire.

They each had a large slice of fruit cake and a mug of coffee laced with whisky.

"Listen to that!" Steve exclaimed as the wind moaned around the house and the rain drummed on the roof. "I reckon we got inside just in time."

They sat in companionable silence while the storm raged outside. The cosy ambience helped them both unwind after the evening's stress.

"I really appreciate you coming out, Em. It would be the last straw if I lost that cow."

As Steve spoke Emma must have noticed how tired and worn he looked.

"I'm just glad I could help." She reached out to hold his hand. "I wish I could do more for you."

"You know I got a letter from Paul Robbins saying he's reviewing my overdraft? If he calls it in . . ." Steve trailed off.

"That's so unfair. Can't you fight him somehow?" Emma fretted.

"Thanks, Em, you're a true friend. But you can't fight the bank. They've got all the big guns and they make the rules."

He slumped down in his chair despondently.

"I don't think anyone can help me. Unless I win Tattslotto or find a gold mine I'm afraid I'm about finished."

He gave a heartfelt sigh as he wrapped his large, work-roughened hand around her slim, soft one.

"I'm sorry, Em. I'm guessing you'd like us to be more than friends, but I can't think about romance with all this hanging over Coolabah.

"Besides, I don't want to drag you into my troubles and mess up our friendship."

Vindicated!

A FEW days before Christmas Celia came to stay with Mandy for the holidays. Carl remained in Melbourne to complete some work. He'd join them on New Year's Eve.

Celia and Mandy sat on the veranda enjoying a drink and the cooling breeze that had sprung up after another hot day.

"You'll never guess what happened at work just before we closed for Christmas." Celia gave Mandy an innocent look. "Morgan Bailey got his marching orders."

"What? The Dragon gone?" Mandy asked, incredulous to hear this news about her former supervisor. "He's been there for ever! Whatever happened?"

"Well, you know how we always thought he bent the rules for Jane?"

"Yes. His pet!"

"Seems she was more than his pet. They were having a full-on affair. Anyway, the board found out and investigated.

"They discovered all sorts of things, including that he'd framed you for stealing and had fired you to cover for Jane, who took the petty cash."

"What a rotter! I hope I get an apology."

"I think you'll get both an apology and an

offer of compensation as soon as the board sort out a few things. Maybe they'll even decide to take you back."

"An apology would be nice and compensation even better. But I won't go back there no matter what they offer me. I'm settled in Whixley now."

Celia gave a cheeky grin.

"I always thought you were a city girl but now I see you're a country girl at heart. Maybe there's more than the job attracting you to Whixley, though. I wish you luck on all fronts."

Celia pointed across to Coolabah, where Steve and Emma were standing close together, leaning on the stockyard fence.

"Those two look cosy."

Seeing the easy familiar relationship between the couple Mandy felt a twinge of jealousy. Celia caught her friend's eye.

"You're not jealous, are you?"

"Of course not," Mandy retorted. "I've got Larry, and Steve's known Emma since they were at school together.

"But I really like Emma and I wish them well."

Celia gave Mandy a quizzical look.

"Hmm. All I know is, if I had to choose between Steve and Larry I'd take Steve any day."

"You Think I'm A Crook?"

MANDY returned to work on the second Tuesday of January. She was surprised when Frank failed to come in as he hadn't mentioned taking additional holidays.

Still, he was the boss and not accountable to her if he took an extra day or two off.

The practice secretary had taken the week off to visit family interstate so Mandy was kept busy before she met Larry after work.

"I don't know when Frank will be fit for work," Larry told her. "The poor old bloke is in hospital after a Christmas binge. But I'm sure you'll be able to handle the business without him," he assured her.

"I did wonder," Mandy replied. "Well, this is being thrown in at the deep end!"

"You'll be fine. I know I can trust you with my business," Larry said confidently.

"Thanks for the vote of confidence. I hope I'm up to it."

Over the next few days, Mandy became concerned when she found several matters that Frank appeared to have mishandled.

They included some of Larry's business, which she brought to his attention.

"I think Frank has reached his 'use by date'." Larry grinned. "So here's your chance to show your stuff and fix all this."

"Larry, I can't just take over Frank's practice. And you can't force him to retire!"

"Let's just say that, if I took my business away from Frank, he wouldn't have much left. Besides, if I told a few of the things he's done he probably wouldn't be allowed to practice anyway," Larry replied in his usual, self-confident manner.

"Larry, that sounds like blackmail! I trust you won't do anything illegal," Mandy protested, feeling distinctly uneasy.

"Don't worry, darling; I'm a businessman, not a crook."

Larry went on to assure Mandy that he'd simply urge Frank to retire now before his drinking got him into real trouble.

She wasn't persuaded but decided not to push the matter further at present. Instead she'd keep a close watch on what was being done in the Whixley Legal Practice now she'd be responsible for the work.

* * * *

After work on her second Friday back Mandy was in the Railway Hotel with Larry.

The weather had been hot and dry since November and today there was a gusty, northerly wind. Consequently a day of Total Fire Ban had been declared for all of Victoria.

An Extreme Fire Danger warning had been issued for northern areas including the Whixley district.

"We could be in trouble if that fire in the hills spreads," Larry remarked as they settled into the armchairs in his office.

"We're safe down here in the valley aren't we?" Mandy asked, a note of concern in her voice. "It's not as though we're up there in the hills, in the bush."

"We're safer," Larry replied. "But if a fire gets near the valley it could spread quickly, particularly with all the long dry grass that's about this year.

"And especially where some of the tree changers haven't cleaned up their blocks."

No doubt seeing how worried Mandy was, Larry reassured her by insisting the fire was a long way from Whixley.

Hearing this she relaxed and turned to the other matter on her mind.

"I don't want to be critical, Larry, but I've noticed some matters concerning your business appear to be questionable, if not borderline illegal."

"What do you mean?" Larry asked sharply.

She noticed his expression cloud over, becoming hard and closed.

"I found some e-mails and payments to Paul Robbins and Sean McAlpine that seem to be, well, questionable."

"What do you mean by questionable? Do you think I'm a crook?"

A familiar harsh edge had crept into his voice.

"No, well, I certainly hope not!" Mandy replied in a conciliatory tone. "It's just one of my colleagues in Melbourne had a case where a land developer was bribing and pressuring a bank manager and a council planning officer.

"The developer ended up in gaol. I don't want to see you get into trouble, that's all."

"I don't intend to end up in gaol. I'm a businessman, not a crook, Mandy. Sometimes I have to make tough decisions."

Seeing her doubtful look, Larry shrugged.

"OK, I'll speak to Frank and find out what he's been up to. You know he's getting old and, what with his drinking, maybe he's been a bit sloppy with some of my business."

The sudden wailing of the town's fire siren curtailed any further discussion. A man rushed into the hotel.

"The fire has jumped the containment lines and it's starting spot fires along Marston Road!" he shouted.

"Marston Road? I live there!" Mandy cried, jumping up. "I've got to get home and make sure my cat's safe.

"I only got him for Christmas and he's just getting settled!"

The fire had started several days ago with a lightning strike in the hills away to the north-west.

Now, it seemed, the hot strong gusty wind was driving it relentlessly toward Whixley. The scorching northerly wind felt like the blast from a furnace.

The conflagration was leaping through the tree tops in the foothills ten kilometres away. Flying embers were now starting spot fires in the grass around the new houses along Marston Road.

These fires were sending up billows of thick, choking smoke as they consumed the dry grass like a ravenous giant.

Mandy and Larry raced out to his car and he drove rapidly out along Marston Road until they were stopped from going further by a road block.

All they could see ahead of them was billowing smoke and leaping flames.

Fire Damage

SORRY, mate, this road is closed to everyone except authorised vehicles," one of the two State Emergency Services volunteers manning the barrier said politely but firmly to Larry.

The man, who normally managed Whixley Farm Supplies, right now wore orange SES coveralls and a protective hard hat.

"But my house is just up ahead, and I've got to make sure my cat is safe!" Mandy cried.

"I'm sorry, love, we can't let you through."

This came from the other SES volunteer, an older woman who'd been widowed a few years ago and now ran a home cleaning service. She also wore the distinctive coveralls and hard hat.

"Even if we did let you through there's nothing you can do. You'd only get in the way of the firies and distract them from fighting the fire. You would be a danger to them and yourselves."

"I suppose so," Mandy conceded reluctantly.

"That's right, love," the woman continued in a kindly tone. "You'll just have to leave the firies to it. They're trained and they've got the proper protective gear.

"Why don't you go back to town? You'll be safe there and you should be able to get through later this evening," she advised.

"Come on, Mandy," Larry instructed. "We can't do anything here.

"Even if they did let us through we wouldn't be able to see anything with all that smoke. I don't fancy being barbequed if we get stuck!

"We'd better get back to town and make sure we've got food and drink ready for everybody when they have finished here."

Mandy was still worried but reluctantly accepted Larry's advice.

Back at the Railway Hotel Mandy threw herself into helping with the preparations for the expected rush of firefighters and others who were expected once the fire was dealt with.

At least she could do something to help and keep her mind off what may be happening at her place.

Although Larry hadn't joined the local Volunteer Fire Brigade he was preparing to put on free beer and meals for the volunteers once the fire danger had passed.

"Sure, it'll cost me a bit, but it'll also get the hotel and me a lot of good PR," Larry expalined grinning, always one to take advantage of a situation.

She was too worried and busy to make much of his words just then, but later they would come back to her. Along with the memory of Emma's observation.

"Larry's in business for Larry."

Around eight Emma herself dropped in to see Mandy. She was between calls to check animals in the fire affected area.

"The good news is that the fire appears to have missed your place," she was able to tell Mandy.

"Thank you so much, Emma. I only hope Tibbles is OK," Mandy replied, feeling relief but still worrying.

"Cats usually try to keep away from danger. He should be right as long as he stays inside," Emma said.

Mandy noticed how tired she looked with a sooty smear across her face. Her usual subtle perfume had been replaced by the reek of fire.

"Why don't you sit here?" Mandy indicated a quiet corner table. "You look like you could do with a break and I know I could.

"I'll get us some coffee and sangers."

"Thanks, Mandy. A little break would be good. I'll just go get some water from the bar."

Emma went over to the bar and got a jug

of water and two glasses. Then she sat down and took a long drink.

Mandy returned a few minutes later and set down two large coffees and a plate of sandwiches on the table before she sat opposite Emma.

"I suppose you've been working flat out," she commiserated.

"Sure have," Emma said before reaching for a sandwich and taking a bite. "Thankfully no houses have been lost, although we had a couple of close calls and a few sheds have gone."

She tucked into the food.

"You're a lifesaver, Mandy. I didn't know I was so hungry until now!"

Mandy gave her time to eat another sandwich and to drink a mouthful of coffee before pressing for more information.

"Is the fire out yet?"

"It's pretty well under control now but it's still burning in several places," Emma replied while she picked up another sandwich. "It jumped the road along from your place and now it's slowly burning down into the valley.

"The real test will come when the southerly change hits us, any time now. That can be a mixed blessing"

"Why is that?"

"The hot, northerly wind usually pushes a

fire fast but on a narrow front.

"With a change the wind swings around about 90 degrees and the fire can then take off on a very wide front. The cooler conditions make fighting the fire easier, but the wider front can mean a whole lot more fire to fight. At least in the short term," Emma finished.

"Does that mean my place still isn't safe?" Mandy asked fearfully.

"No-one's really safe until the fire is out," Emma answered. "But your place should be OK."

* * * *

By midnight the fire was out and Marston Road had been reopened. As tired, hungry firefighters and Emergency Services workers began to fill the hotel Mandy excused herself and went to check on her home.

"I have to go and make sure Tibbles is safe," she told Larry who was busy laying out free beer and meals.

"If you wait a little while I'll come with you," he told her.

But she was impatient to check her place as soon as possible and, in particular, to check on her cat. So she left immediately with Larry promising to come along when he could.

Outside, the smell of smoke was very

noticeable compared to inside where the air-conditioning reduced it. Mandy drove rapidly out along Marston Road and in the bright moonlight saw a couple of fire trucks still patrolling to deal with any remaining hot spots.

She rejoiced to see that the wattle trees along the roadside near her driveway had escaped the fire.

Her heart was thumping as she turned into her driveway, dreading what she might find. However, thankfully, there was no obvious damage to her house or garden, although the bright moonlight revealed large dark blotches where the fire had come perilously close.

It had been stopped short of the house and garden.

Emma's advice to have the long grass around her house slashed at the beginning of summer and to plant fire-resistant bushes in her garden had without doubt helped the firefighters stop the fire before it reached her house.

Tibbles was now her only worry.

On leaving her car Mandy was hit with a strong smell of smoke and the distinctive smell of burned gum leaves. These had been sucked down from the hills, where the fire had raged amongst the tall eucalypts for several days.

"Tibbles! Here puss, puss," Mandy called anxiously as she opened her front door.

She was overjoyed when Tibbles strolled up to greet her and rubbed around her legs.

He looked up and meowed indignantly as if to say, "About time you came home. I'm starving."

"Sorry I'm late," Mandy said, reaching down to pick him up. "I know you must be hungry but thank goodness you're all right. I got here as soon as I could."

While she spoke she cuddled the cat and went to the fridge to get his food.

Soon Tibbles was purring loudly and tucking into his meal while Mandy phoned Larry.

"Yes, I got home safely.

"No, the fire didn't come up to the house, but it came very close.

"That's OK. I understand you're busy," Mandy finished flatly. "Anyway, I'm tired so I'll see you tomorrow."

She turned from her phone, disappointed that Larry wouldn't be coming out as he'd promised.

"But then, I can't expect him to drop everything for me," she told herself as she prepared a long, luxurious bath before going to bed.

Once there she was quickly asleep and slept soundly, emotionally and physically exhausted, until the raucous calls from a flock of white cockatoos wheeling and screeching overhead woke her next morning.

After breakfast Mandy went outside. The stale smell of burning lay heavy in the air and her house and garden were an unburned island in a wide sea of blackened ground.

She looked across towards the Coolabah homestead and saw that a tentacle of fire had reached right down to the creek. The old shed which previously stood on the Coolabah side was now a heap of blackened timbers and twisted roofing-iron.

Some fencing would need to be replaced, but otherwise her own property was undamaged.

Thank goodness for the Volunteer Fire Brigade.

Mandy's heart overflowed with gratitude to the men and women who'd saved her home.

"I must see about joining up as soon as I can," she vowed. "I don't want to just benefit from living here; I want to be part of the community and contribute to it."

Playing Fair

ON Monday evening Mandy and Emma were sitting on Mandy's front veranda chatting over drinks.

"I can't thank you enough, Emma. Your advice about cutting the grass and planting fire-resistant things in the garden paid off." Mandy surveyed the blackened areas still clearly visible around her house and garden.

"I wish some of the other tree changers would get the message," Emma replied. "It puts us all in danger when people don't clean up their property.

"Hopefully some lessons have been learned, especially by people like that family further along Marston Road. The long grass plus inflammable things in their garden meant the Fire Brigade had to work really hard to save their place," she concluded.

"Speaking about the Fire Brigade, I've enquired about joining up," Mandy told her. "I want to give something back."

"That's great news, Mandy! You're becoming a real part of the community and you'll help to make a difference."

"Make a real difference for real people," Mandy said to herself.

That was why she'd moved out of the city.

"Do you realise, next Friday is Australia Day and it'll be a year since I came here with Mum and Dad." Mandy passed a bowl of crisps to Emma. "Try these, they're a new flavour I got in Melbourne yesterday."

"Mmm, they are yummy," Emma said taking a handful. "How are your parents and how was their trip?"

"They had a fantastic time. They got back last week. Would you believe they travelled nearly twenty thousand kilometres? That's further than from here to London!"

"That's some trip!" Emma replied. "I'd like to travel, but I'll have to wait a while before I can take that much time off work."

"The advantages of retiring with a good pension!" Mandy chuckled and topped up their drinks. "But, then, they've worked for a long time to be in that position."

The young women sat back in their chairs and a peaceful silence fell.

"Did I tell you they're coming to visit next week?" Mandy asked after a while.

"That's great, I'll look forward to meeting them." Emma reached for more crisps. "These are so moreish. You'd better put them out of reach before I scoff the lot!"

Some time ago Emma had told Mandy that she and Steve had been friends since they were at school together.

"A lot of people thought we'd end up

together. For a while I did, too, but now I realise we're really more like sister and brother than girlfriend and boyfriend," Emma said with a wry laugh.

"I've told you, though, that Brian and I were becoming more attracted to each other? Well, guess what happened last night!"

Without waiting for an answer she rushed on.

"He asked me to marry him." Emma tried to sound casual but was unable to hide her excitement.

"And?" Mandy asked.

"Of course I said yes!" Emma's eyes sparkled and her voice rang with joy. "I'm certain Brian's the man for me."

"Congratulations, Emma. Brian's a really good guy. I'm so happy for you.

"I think you're a great match and I wish you every happiness," Mandy said warmly and she moved to embrace her friend.

"I'm a bit envious, though. You're so certain Brian and you are meant for each other.

"While I'm attracted to Larry in many ways I can't shake off this nagging feeling that something isn't quite right. Do you think I'm being silly, or unreasonable?"

"I think you're right to be cautious, Mandy. Larry has a lot of good points and he's done a lot for this district, but it seems that, whatever he does, it's always Larry first, somewhere along the line.

"Take the way he put on free beer for the firefighters and others at the Railway after the fire. A good deed, yes, but it was also good PR for him and the hotel.

"I don't want to sound like a whinger but it also took business away from Brian at the Commercial. He doesn't have Larry's other sources of income to subsidise that sort of thing."

"I just thought Larry was being generous, but when you put it that way . . ." Mandy said thoughtfully. "I suppose the two hotels are competitors."

"And that's OK – as long as its fair competition," Emma replied. "I'm sorry, but I don't think Larry always plays fair."

Mandy sat quietly considering Emma's words.

Larry Lawson, local land developer and landlord of the Railway Hotel, had played a big role in her life ever since she'd come to Whixley. Over the past year they had grown close, but . . .

Yes, there were some serious buts about Larry.

Aunt Clara's Trunk

MANDY was about to leave for work when her phone rang. It was a courier advising he had a delivery for her and shortly he arrived.

"A family heirloom, eh?" the driver enquired as he unloaded a slightly battered tin trunk. "Where d'ya want it?"

"In here, please." Mandy opened the door to her spare room.

She signed the delivery docket and the driver departed, leaving her gazing at the trunk.

It was about 1.2 metres long and 60 centimetres wide and deep.

There was a sturdy fold-down handle on each end and the hinged lid was fastened with two leather straps and a locked catch.

The trunk had been mentioned particularly in Aunt Clara's will and Mandy had eagerly anticipated receiving it.

Now it was here!

The estate lawyer had told Mandy it contained a wedding dress. This was strange as Aunt Clara had never married, to Mandy's knowledge.

Mandy was bursting with curiosity.

"Just time for a quick peek," she told herself, glancing at her watch. "Pity I've got that appointment in half an hour."

Without delay Mandy found the key the lawyer had posted to her. Her excitement bubbled as she lifted the lid.

The first thing she saw was the carefully folded, white lace dress.

Underneath it was a large, antique family bible and some neatly bundled letters or papers.

Sitting among them was Aunt Clara's jewellery box which the lawyer had arranged to ship in the trunk.

Mandy removed a few items and found that the bottom of the trunk was filled with photo albums and back issues of "The Kalgoorlie Miner", the local newspaper.

Wishing she had time for a proper look Mandy reluctantly closed the trunk and headed off to work.

"Never mind," she consoled herself, "I'll finish early and check it out."

Her plan to do so was frustrated when an urgent matter that required considerable work came up just as she was ready to leave.

By the time it was sorted she barely had time for a quick meal at the Railway Hotel before crossing the road to the Commercial where the Fire Brigade Information Meeting was taking place.

"Good to see you," Emma greeted Mandy

as she came into the meeting-room.

"I only just made it," Mandy replied. "I had to work late and barely had time to grab a bite to eat before I came here."

"That's the way it goes when you're flying solo!" Emma said with a laugh.

Mandy considered this. She liked "flying solo" as Emma put it.

She only wished she didn't have those questions about Frank's work.

Her thoughts were interrupted by a call for everybody to take their seats.

As they moved to their places Mandy looked around at the people gathered. They numbered around 50.

"How many here tonight are already in the Brigade, Em?"

"About 15," Emma told her. "It's really good to see so many of our newer residents here. I'm guessing the fire gave them a scare."

"I know it gave me a scare!" Mandy said as they found chairs near the front.

A big man with a pleasant, open face stood up.

"Looks like Freddo's ready to start," Emma said.

"Good evening and welcome," the man began. "I'm Nathan Frederickson, generally known as Freddo. I'm our local Volunteer Fire Brigade captain.

"Thank you for coming along tonight. This meeting has two purposes. First, we want to share some things you can all do to reduce the danger of fire, both to your own properties and to the district.

"Then we'll tell you a bit about our local Fire Brigade and invite you to consider joining and helping to protect us all."

When Freddo spoke about cutting long grass and planting fire-resistant gardens Mandy nudged Emma, remembering how this advice had helped save her property.

"Thank you for listening," Freddo concluded 20 minutes later. "One last thing before we have supper – could everyone who wants to attend the Introductory Fire Brigade Training next Wednesday please put your name on the list on the table over there?

"Remember. Men, women, young, old, we've got jobs for you all."

Mandy was among over a dozen prospective firefighters who put their names on the list.

Losing Coolabah

RUSTY, old mate, it's the end of the line. The end of 150 years of Jacksons at Coolabah Flats.

"Others beat their problems but I don't reckon we can beat this."

Steve slumped in his chair, a letter dangling from his hand.

Rusty licked the hand and then sat with his head cocked. His long, pink tongue lolled from the side of his mouth as he panted in the late January summer heat.

He was a loyal friend but he couldn't understand why his beloved master was so bereft.

"If I only knew who's been complaining to the council, Rusty, I would talk to them, set them straight.

"And why are the bank and the council changing the rules and trying so hard to make it impossible for me to keep Coolabah?"

Before he sank into further depression Steve's thoughts were interrupted by the arrival of a familiar 4WD ute.

Rusty ran out, tail wagging nineteen to the dozen, to greet the visitors.

"You seem a bit down in the mouth, old

son," Rick commented as he and Don approached Steve, who remained slumped in his chair on the homestead veranda.

"G'day," Steve greeted them. "Sorry I'm such a misery today. Grab a beer and pull up a pew."

Steve indicated the nearby fridge and chairs.

When they were seated Steve showed them the letter he had received that morning.

Paul Robbins was giving him 14 days to clear his overdraft or the bank would commence proceedings to take possession of Coolabah.

Rick handed the letter back.

"That's a bit rough, mate," he commented in the understated Australian way.

Steve was too dispirited to reply.

"If you want my advice," Don said, "just accept Lawson's offer, take the money and run. Buy another place further out."

"I know that'd be the easy way out, Don. But my family have owned Coolabah since the pioneer days and I don't want to be the one to lose it all.

"Besides, I don't want that Lawson character to win."

"True, Steve, but this area's changing," Don replied. "Look how Smethurst's place across the valley has been cut up. And now your other neighbour has sold to Lawson."

"I know all that. Thing is, I just want to be left alone, to get on with farming and let others get on with whatever.

"But how can I with those complaints to the council and now this letter from Robbins?

"It's almost like someone is deliberately trying to force me out!" he finished indignantly.

"I bet Lawson's behind it somehow. I wouldn't trust him or his lawyer mate, Barty, as far as I could kick 'em," Rick added with feeling. "As for Robbins, I reckon he's even worse than those other two."

"Why is that, Rick?" Don wanted to know.

"Well, land developers and lawyers, you almost expect they'll be a bit suss, don't you?" Rick replied. "But you expect better from bank managers. Aren't they supposed to be pillars of society?"

"That's a good point, Rick," Don replied thoughtfully. "I s'pose you can't tar all land developers, lawyers and bank managers with the same brush, but we do seem to have a rum lot here in Whixley."

"I'm sure there's something going on!" Rick continued. "When I was in the bank the other day there was quite a blue in the manager's office.

"Lawson was yelling 'Just get it done pronto'. And when Robbins came out he looked pretty upset."

Steve frowned, then shrugged.

"Well, I'm sorry, but you boys have wasted your trip out here today. Thanks to this letter I'll have to can any more work on that fencing job.

"I'll pay for what you've done so far, but then . . ." he trailed off.

"That's OK, cobber," Rick said quickly. "Can't leave a mate's job half done and you'll pay us when you can. Right, Don?"

"Sure thing," Don replied. "We've got the materials and there's only about three hours' work left. We should knock it over this arvo."

"You're proper mates," Steve said. "I'll make this up to you somehow."

"No worries. And, despite what you might say about Larry Lawson, he gives us a lot of work with all his new subdivisions," Don replied in a conciliatory tone as he went to get his tools.

They were soon busy with Steve's fencing job and it was finished by late afternoon.

As they tidied up their tools, mulling over the changes in the area, they agreed that Larry had indeed brought a lot of welcome money to the district.

But they weren't so happy about some of the accompanying changes.

* * * *

That evening Steve had dinner with his cousin Brian.

"I'm sorry, Steve, I'd like to help if I could," Brian said when Steve showed him the bank's letter. "I'm fully extended just now with all the pub renovations.'

"That's OK. I wasn't looking for a loan or anything; I just needed to talk to someone.

"By the way, don't you think it's strange we've both got problems with Paul Robbins threating to cut off our credit, even though our loans aren't behind? And now the council are trying to renege on our permits?"

A thought struck him.

"You haven't had an offer from Lawson or anyone else wanting to buy the hotel?"

"Funny you should mention that. I did receive a call from some bloke in Melbourne a while ago. Said he was acting for some trust or something.

"I told him the Commercial wasn't for sale. Then, a couple of days ago, Dad got a letter with an offer to buy us out.

"It was quite a generous offer, but the pub's been in our family since the early days and we want to keep it that way."

"You don't know who made the offers?"

"No. Probably some Melbourne investor who's seen how Whixley's growing and wants to get a piece of the action."

"That's the problem," Steve said morosely. "Town starts going ahead and all these outsiders want to get a share."

"On a brighter note it's good to see Coolabah escaped the fire." Brian went to the fridge for two more beers.

"Thank goodness for small blessings," Steve replied with a wry grin as he opened his stubbie. "I only lost that old shed down by the creek. There was nothing in it, but now I'll have to clean it up sometime."

They fell silent.

Steve sighed.

"The only hope I can see is to win Tattslotto or find a goldmine."

"Didn't your family have a goldmine at one time?"

"Yes, in the hills at the back of Coolabah. I was reading about it in my great-great-grandmother's diary the other day.

"It seems the gold they found saved Coolabah in the 1890s when the banks were in trouble and credit dried up. I could sure use some of that gold now!"

Their meals arrived.

"This steak's really good," Steve said a

while later as he cut another slice.

"It should be." Brian grinned. "It's from one of your Wagyu steers."

They finished their meals.

"The goldmine's not all I found in Great-great-grandma's diary. In 1895 her younger son, Ian, vanished. He'd been working the mine with a couple of hired hands, but the mine closed not long before Ian left.

"My great-great-grandfather reckoned Ian had been stockpiling the last of the gold and took it when he left. He probably thought of it as his share of the inheritance.

"His mother didn't believe he took the gold. Ian was her favourite though he didn't get on with his father."

"Gee, that's quite a story. What happened to Ian after he left?"

"I don't know. He just disappeared."

"Another one?" Brian asked.

"No, thanks, Brian. I've got to drive home. Actually, there was a rumour that Ian went to the West but the family never heard from him again.

"I wonder what happened to him – and how many rellies I might have that I'll never know."

Too Trusting

SURE, I'm happy to provide legal advice,"
Mandy told Freddo over supper the
following Wednesday evening.

A dozen new volunteers had just
completed their first training session with
Freddo in the large tin shed that served as
the Whixley Fire Station.

Mandy had thoroughly enjoyed the
evening.

"But I want to be fully involved," she told
the officer. "I want to learn all I can about
fire-fighting and do my bit as a 'hands on'
firefighter."

"That's great, Mandy." Freddo reached
for another piece of cake. "Ah, nothing
beats Mrs Turner's fruit cake.

"We want everyone to be fully involved
and trained so they can help when there's a
fire or other emergency," he continued.
"When it comes to people like you with
particular skills, we want to use those skills
to benefit the community."

Later, Mandy snuggled into her bed
enfolded by warm feelings as she reflected
on how good it was to be part of the
community and work together.

The opportunity to make a real difference

for real people was especially rewarding because, after all, wasn't that why she'd moved to Whixley?

It really had been the right decision.

Then a cold chill hit her. What about those matters she'd found in Frank's files?

The more she uncovered in the lawyer's office, the more all these questionable actions seemed to have been done to benefit Larry Lawson.

Conflicting thoughts jostled and tangled in Mandy's mind. Had Larry properly explained the matters she'd raised with him before their talk had been cut short by the fire?

At best there were unanswered questions. At worst . . . no. She didn't want to go down that road.

There was no denying she owed Larry a great deal and she really wanted to give him the benefit of the doubt.

But she was a lawyer, someone who dealt in facts. And there were facts that definitely needed explaining.

Then there was Frank Barty.

Had he been doing the wrong thing or were these discrepancies merely the result of his alcoholic bumbling, as Larry had suggested?

Frank was an experienced solicitor and most of these matters appeared to be deliberate and calculated actions, not simple incompetence.

Even if Frank's drinking was the problem these matters must be fixed before they got out of hand and led to serious consequences.

But what should she do?

"I'll keep my eyes open, conduct a proper investigation and make notes," Mandy told herself as her lawyer mind kicked in before she fell into a restless, broken sleep.

* * * *

On Thursday Mandy woke late, feeling jaded.

She had taken the day off so that, with the Australia Day holiday tomorrow, she'd have a four-day weekend to host her parents plus Celia and Carl, who had also taken time off work.

"I hope I'm not coming down with something," Mandy muttered as she reluctantly got out of bed and went to the bathroom.

"Goodness, I'm late!" she exclaimed on returning and checking her bedside clock. "Better get moving."

By the time Celia and Carl arrived around mid-morning Mandy had picked up and felt much better as she served morning tea on her front veranda.

"I don't think I'll ever get tired of this view." Celia stretched back in her chair with a long contented sigh and let her sparkling brown eyes drink in the vista, down along the valley and across to Coolabah.

"I know how you feel, Celia. Everything here is just what I hoped for. Well, almost everything," Mandy finished in a barely audible whisper.

"Oh?" Celia queried. "Not boyfriend troubles with Larry?"

"Not exactly. But he's involved."

"I think you'd better tell us the whole story." Carl had been sitting by quietly. "You know they say a problem shared is a problem halved."

Mandy hesitated, unwilling to burden her friends with her concerns about Larry and Frank. But with a little gentle prodding the whole story spilled out.

"I really think you'd be better off without Larry," Celia decided firmly at the end. "I'm sorry, Mandy, but that is my considered opinion."

"I think Celia's right," Carl agreed, fixing his dark eyes on Mandy. "The more immediate consideration is your career, of course, Mandy."

"What do mean, my career?" Mandy asked with a stab of concern.

"Don't be naïve. You're a lawyer; don't be

too trusting or your career could be in danger.

"Frank Barty might have done, or not done, things that could lead to disciplinary action. If you work with him for much longer you risk being implicated in whatever mess he may have created."

Carl's blunt assessment shocked Mandy into silence and she remembered Frank's own warning not to let Larry get a hold on her.

Did Larry already have a hold on her?

"I'm sorry to be so blunt," Carl told her gently. "But I don't want to see you dragged into someone else's mess."

"That's OK, Carl. I know you only want to help and I'm glad it's all out now.

"The problem is, to use a good old legal term, I'm afraid I've got a conflict of interest. Or should that be conflicts of interest?"

"You know we only have your best interests at heart," Celia said, reaching to squeeze Mandy's hand.

"That's right," Carl added. "Loyalty is all very well, but if it pushes you into a situation where you're breaking the law then you need to think carefully about that loyalty.

"You need a plan; you need to build a case. If there are indeed irregularities you'll have to decide what action to take."

"And we'll be there to help and support you all the way, won't we, Carl?"

"Naturally," Carl replied.

"You're right, Carl." Mandy brightened up. "I feel a lot better knowing you and Celia are with me."

"A few copies of relevant papers would be helpful," Carl observed. "But I'd make sure the practice secretary doesn't know what you're doing in case she tells Frank or Larry.

"Above all, make sure you are not involved in any questionable actions," he concluded.

Mandy nodded.

"The secretary only works part time so that shouldn't be a problem," she replied as her phone rang.

She turned to her friends.

"It's Mum. They're about fifteen minutes away."

"Better get the barbie fired up, then," Carl said, getting to his feet.

Telling Tales

HALF an hour later the happy party was enjoying Carl's efforts from the barbecue.

"This steak is really good; so tender and juicy!" Clive stood up to get another piece.

"Must be thanks to the cook," Carl, ever the joker, quipped with an exaggerated show of modesty.

"Mandy, didn't you say these steaks are from Steve Jackson's Wagyu cattle?" Celia queried.

"They sure are."

"Then that must be why they're so good," Celia said, giving Carl a friendly dig in the ribs and a mischievous smile just as a small bright blue SUV arrived.

"Look, it's Emma and Brian!" Mandy cried happily, standing to greet them. "I'm so glad they could come."

"Sorry we're a bit late," Emma apologised when Mandy ran forward. "Had a minor emergency with a dog this morning. Nothing too serious and it's all fixed now."

"The penalty for working solo," Mandy quoted as she brought her friends forward to introduce her parents.

"Well, making a real difference for people makes it all worthwhile," Emma replied.

"I see you've got some of Steve's Wagyu steaks," Brian observed as he tucked into the perfectly done steak Carl served him. "They're very popular with our hotel diners. The health-conscious customers reckon all that good fat provides health benefits."

The conversation turned to Mandy's parents' recent trip around Australia and the great time they'd had.

"It was so good that our six-month trip ended up being closer to a year!" Merrill confessed. "I never imagined living in a caravan for so long, but now I'm looking forward to some time at home."

They chatted on until Clive pushed his empty plate and glass aside.

"I'd better go and set up the caravan."

Mandy explained where to park the caravan and Carl and Brian went to help.

The women remained on the veranda. Merrill could no longer contain her worry as she observed how tired and drawn her daughter looked.

"Is everything all right, love?"

"I'm OK, Mum," Mandy replied quickly. Too quickly, Merrill thought.

"I'm a bit tired. I've had a lot on at work."

Merrill was prevented from asking more as Carl returned with a question and Mandy went to assist with parking the caravan.

Once she was out of earshot Merrill

turned to Celia.

"I don't want to pry, but I'm worried. You're Mandy's friend, Celia. Tell me honestly, is she really all right?"

"I don't want to tell tales," Celia began, torn between loyalty to her friend and believing Mandy needed help.

"I admire your loyalty but I'm her mother. I can't help if I don't know what's wrong."

Celia drew a deep breath.

"It's Larry Lawson. He's been a great help with her move and she likes him, but . . ."

Ah, boyfriend troubles, Merrill thought, relieved it was nothing more serious.

Mandy and the men returned just then so Merrill didn't pursue the matter any further.

Celia was relieved. She didn't want to burden Merrill with suspicions about Larry's business activities.

Nor did she want to tell Merrill that her daughter might be involved, even if only by association, in some possibly illegal activities.

"Well, Mandy, you've a magnificent property here," Clive commented.

He sat down and Carl handed him a beer.

"I could almost be persuaded to move here myself, but I doubt I could get your mother to leave the city," he finished with a chuckle.

"Thanks, Dad," Mandy answered while

her mother just smiled. "Do you know this place used to be part of Coolabah?

"The Jacksons were one of the first families to settle in the district and they still own the other side of the creek."

She pointed across the valley to where Steve could be seen moving around his cattle yards, a little way from the substantial old, red brick homestead.

"So that's where our steak comes from!" Clive observed. "I've read about Wagyu beef, but I've never actually tasted it before today.

"Now I have to agree with those who say there seems to be a good future for farmers who do it right, although I understand it requires a lot of capital to get started."

"You're not wrong about the capital that's needed," Brian told him.

"Steve was able to get finance from the bank but now the local manager, Paul Robbins, wants to renege on the deal and call Steve's loan in and force him off Coolabah."

"If a loan is behind then the bank has to protect its interest, otherwise no-one would repay their loans," Clive said. "The bank would go out of business and we'd all lose out."

"True, but Steve's not behind with his repayments," Brian answered.

"Your loan's not behind, either," Emma added emphatically. "And Paul Robbins wants to call it in, too.

"There's something shonky about that bank, no wonder people want the Barton Community Bank to open a branch in Whixley," she concluded, referring to the very successful, community-owned bank in the nearby larger town.

"That doesn't sound right," Clive remarked.

"Dad ought to know," Mandy said. "He used to be a Senior Bank Manager."

"Then maybe he can do something about Paul Robbins?" Emma said.

"I'd be concerned if what you say is true," Clive replied. "That's not the way the bank expects responsible managers to behave."

"It's not only how he's treating Brian and Steve," Emma continued. "It's really bad the way he bullies the young woman who works with him."

"Hmm, seems I've already got my first job for that Special Investigations Consultancy the bank have asked me to take on," Clive replied, pulling out his notebook and pen.

Clara And Curley

LOOKS like another warm one," Clive observed as Brian and Steve called at eight the next morning to collect him and Carl for the day's fishing they'd arranged.

"True, but it'll be good sitting in the shade out by the river with a few cold tinnies while we wait for the fish," Brian promised.

"I haven't been fishing for years! Hope I haven't lost my touch." Clive grinned.

"And I've never tried it," Carl added.

"Not to worry," Steve told them. "We're going to a place where the fish line up just waiting to be caught!"

"So we expect fresh fish for tea," Mandy quipped while the men climbed into Steve's LandCruiser.

"Have the grill ready," Steve ordered, fastening his seat belt.

"You've got everything you need?" Merrill queried as Steve prepared to drive off.

"I reckon so. The fishing gear is in the back and Brian has stashed the food and drink to keep it cool. And we all know what a top caterer he is."

"Sunscreen and insect repellent?"

"Mum, they're not children," Mandy chided gently.

"All under control." Steve gave Mandy a wink that made her tingle and brought a pink tinge to her cheeks.

It was something that Celia observed with a smile.

Once the men had gone the women relaxed with a cuppa and chatted while admiring the view from Mandy's veranda.

Forty minutes later Emma arrived.

"Now we're all here we can check out Aunt Clara's trunk!" Mandy was full of excitement. "I've been trying to find time to have a proper look."

They pulled the trunk into the lounge, where there was space for them all to gather round, and spread out the contents.

First they carefully unwrapped the wedding dress, which Mandy held up for them to admire.

"I wonder why she had a wedding dress when she never married," Mandy mused as she gently twirled the dress around.

"Maybe it was her mother's," Celia ventured.

"I don't think so." Merrill was examining the dress. "This looks more 1940s than 1920s. Besides, from photos I've seen Clara's mother was quite short.

"This dress would be too long for her even allowing for a floor-length gown. It's for someone more Mandy's height."

"Maybe she had you in mind, Mandy," Celia said with a grin.

"I don't think I'll be needing a wedding dress any time soon," Mandy replied quietly. "On a more positive note, it must be lunchtime and I've some gnocchi and prawn salad in the fridge."

"Maybe there will be something in those papers to help us solve the mystery," Merrill said as they moved to the kitchen.

After lunch they were looking through some of the old Kalgoorlie newspapers from the trunk when Emma gasped.

"Look at this!"

She pointed to a 1942 report about an incident during the Japanese invasion of New Guinea. It described the heroic actions of a Kalgoorlie soldier, Sergeant William "Bluey" Cameron and his Victorian mate, Sergeant Christopher "Curley" Jackson.

The two young soldiers had provided covering fire for their mates when their unit was ambushed by a large enemy force.

Their bravery allowed the other troops to regroup in safety, but sadly Bluey and Curley were overrun before their mates could save them.

Mandy peered at the newspaper image of two smiling young soldiers, taken shortly before they went to New Guinea.

"That's Bluey, Aunt Clara's brother. Look,

it's the same picture Dad has."

"And you told me Steve has a copy in his old family album!" Emma added excitedly.

"Gosh," Merrill said. "Just think, Mandy. You and that nice Steve had great-uncles who served together all those years ago.

"It's a small world. I wonder what else we'll find."

* * * *

Around mid-afternoon Merrill announced afternoon tea, which received an enthusiastic response.

The three girls moved out to the kitchen where Mandy's mum was setting out fresh scones with jam and cream.

"Mmm, you're the best scone-maker, Mum!" Mandy said.

She passed the plate of delicious-smelling scones to Celia and Emma.

"It's a good thing I don't eat here every day!" Emma laughed as she finished another scone. "I'd never fit into my clothes."

"You don't have to worry," Mandy assured her. "You're always on the go! Me, sitting behind a desk all day, that's another story."

They continued with light-hearted banter for a while before returning to the trunk.

Merrill began leafing through the big old

family bible.

"Look, this is addressed to you."

Celia passed Mandy an envelope which she accepted with a puzzled look.

She opened the envelope and the women became quiet and even a little teary as she read Aunt Clara's letter aloud.

It had been written not long before her death. It told how Clara and Curley Jackson had planned to marry when he returned from New Guinea.

The dress had been made in preparation but, of course, Curley didn't return, so the dress was stored away.

So, my dear Mandy, when you read this I'll be gone. I'm leaving you my dress in the hope that you may be able to wear it on your big day, whenever that may be.

"That explains the wedding dress," Celia commented.

Mandy then showed the others an enclosed photo of Curley which was inscribed on the back.

To my darling Clara, with all my love. Can't wait to get back and marry you.

Love Curley.

Family Tree

THE men returned from their fishing trip around five and everyone gathered in the air conditioned comfort of Mandy's kitchen, the lounge room being occupied with the contents of the trunk.

The men's catch of several Redfin and a large Yellow Belly, was enthusiastically received whilst Mandy and Celia set out drinks.

Once they were all served Mandy turned to Steve.

"Hello, cuz!"

"What do you mean?" he asked, casting Mandy a baffled look.

"What I say," she replied with a mischievous grin. "Remember that night, not long after I moved to Whixley, when you rescued me? You told me about Ian Jackson leaving home in the 1890s and how you might have relatives you may never know about.

"Guess what? I'm one of those relatives!"

"You're what? How's that?" Steve shook his head in bewilderment. "Is this some kind of joke?"

"Not at all," Mandy replied demurely.

Carl, Clive and Brian were looking on with

puzzled expressions while the women exchanged amused smiles.

"It's true, I am a distant cousin of yours," Mandy continued. "What's more, I know where Ian went and why your family didn't hear from him."

Merrill was pleased to see her daughter's tension seem to disappear while she teased Steve.

"You'd better tell them, love, before they burst with curiosity," she said.

"It's a long story and we found it all in Aunt Clara's trunk," Mandy began. "You'd better tell the first bit, Mum – you found it."

Merrill explained how she had found the family tree records in Aunt Clara's old family bible.

"The family tree led back to Clive's grandfather, Mandy's great-grandfather. His name was Albert Cameron and he was born in Kalgoorlie in 1897."

"But that's not all!" Mandy interrupted with growing excitement. "Now comes the interesting bit."

She went into the lounge and returned a few seconds later with several of the old "Kalgoorlie Miner" newspapers from the trunk.

"Look at this!" she declared, opening one of the papers on the kitchen table which had been hastily cleared to make room.

Mandy pointed to a report from July 1897 of an accident on a mining claim owned by Angus Cameron, a Scot, and Ian Jackson, lately of Whixley, Victoria.

The report described how twenty-four-year-old Ian, who had married a year earlier, had been seriously injured when a drive he was working in collapsed.

He had been pulled out but, sadly, he died the next day leaving a widow, Dorothy, who was expecting their first child.

"No wonder the family never heard from poor old Ian, then," Steve marvelled. "But how . . .?"

"Ah, here's where it gets really interesting," Mandy cut in. "We also found this."

She took a large old envelope from Celia, who had been holding it for her.

The envelope contained a certificate recording the marriage of Angus Cameron, bachelor, and Dorothy Jackson, widow, in Kalgoorlie on September 10, 1897.

"They didn't waste any time," Carl commented.

"That's how it was back then," Clive answered. "There was no Social Security and the goldfields were no place for a woman on her own, especially if she had a baby. It wasn't unusual for a family member, or a mate, to marry a widow who'd been left alone.

"That way both she and any children would be provided for and the new husband, who may well have been widowed himself, would gain a housekeeper and a mother for any children he might have.

"Marriage for love was a luxury they couldn't always afford to wait for."

"But wait, there's still more!" Mandy said.

Merrill again rejoiced to see Mandy all smiles as, with a flourish, she produced another document.

"This is the birth certificate of Albert Jackson Cameron, born November 8, 1897. His parents are listed as Dorothy and Angus Cameron.

"But, of course, they had only been married for two months. Dorothy had been married to Ian Jackson when Albert was conceived."

"Wow!" Steve exclaimed as light dawned. "So Albert was really Ian Jackson's son."

"And that makes us distant cousins," Mandy finished, grinning at Steve.

Frank Returns

ON the Monday after Australia Day Mandy's
parents prepared to leave. Her mother was
still fussing and worrying about Mandy
despite Celia's attempts to reassure her.

"I wish we could stay longer but Dad's
keen to get home and take up that
consultancy with the bank. I think he's been
missing his work."

She hugged Mandy while Clive gave the
caravan a final check.

"Don't worry, Mum, I'm all right. You and
Dad just enjoy yourselves and we'll catch up
again soon," Mandy replied, trying to
sound bright and cheerful.

By the time her parents left and Mandy
got to work it was after ten. When she
walked in she was both surprised and
relieved to see Frank in reception.

"Welcome back, Frank. It's good to see
you and I hope you're feeling better."

She noted Frank looked anything but
healthy; his sallow face was drawn and he'd
lost weight.

"Thank you," he replied but Mandy
noticed his voice was weaker. "There are
some things we need to catch up on."

He led Mandy into his office and asked the

secretary to hold any calls.

Mandy updated Frank on the matters she'd dealt with during his absence. Most were routine and he seemed happy.

She searched for a way to mention her concerns about some files.

She didn't want to burden Frank who was obviously unwell; however, she needed answers for her own peace of mind, if for nothing else.

Her dilemma was solved when Frank looked up at her.

"Mandy, you're young and bright, talented and hardworking and you've managed the practice very well. You have a promising future.

"Do you remember I warned you to not let Larry Lawson get a hold on you?"

"Yes." She wondered what was coming.

"I did a lot of thinking in hospital. To be blunt, you should get out while you can. I don't want to see Larry ruin your career – like he's ruined mine."

Mandy was confused.

Was Frank trying to get rid of her so Larry couldn't push him out and install her to run the practice, or was he giving her a genuine warning?

Frank saw the doubt in Mandy's eyes and shook his head.

"I'm sorry, Mandy, I know you and Larry

are close. And I'm also aware he can be very charming and generous. But that man is dangerous when things don't go his way."

"I – I'm confused," Mandy stammered. "I need time to think."

The grandfather clock in the corner marked time while they both sat quietly.

When Frank leaned back and closed his eyes Mandy noticed how he sagged and heard his raspy, laboured breathing.

"Thank you for warning me, Frank, and I am grateful for your advice.

"But apart from anything else I can't just up and leave you here, well, at least not until your health improves."

"I appreciate your concern, Mandy, but you must consider your future."

"I know," Mandy replied desperately. "But if I leave, where can I go?

"I don't want to leave Whixley and I can't go back to my old job in the city. I don't think I could do that sort of work again.

"Besides, even though I've now been exonerated, some mud is bound to stick over my dismissal for allegedly stealing from the company!"

An Ugly Meeting

LARRY was in a meeting later that day with Frank, Paul Robbins and Sean McAlpine. The others were struggling to convince him to back off from trying to buy Coolabah.

"At least until things blow over," Sean counselled.

"I didn't get where I am by backing down," Larry retorted.

"Larry, you don't understand the pressure I'm under," Paul whined, "especially now Mandy's father and the regional manager are investigating me."

"That's your problem, deal with it," Larry replied with chilling calmness.

"I could lose my job. And if that proposal for a community bank in Whixley goes ahead this branch will be downgraded, maybe even closed.

"I'll probably have to leave town. I'll be of no use to you then!" Paul concluded with a spark of defiance.

"You're no use to me now if you can't get Jackson off Coolabah!" Larry replied harshly. "Just finish this job and I'll pay you out, then we can part company."

The planning officer, who'd been sitting by while Larry berated Paul, stepped up.

"Larry, you need to forget about Coolabah, at least until this council investigation blows over."

"You wimping out on me, too, Sean?"

"Of course not," he replied smoothly. "But I can't push too hard on those permits for Jackson and the pub until the council investigation is wrapped up."

"Let's keep it all civil," Frank said with his usual attempt to keep the peace. "Maybe you should get out while you're ahead."

"I didn't get where I am by quitting," Larry repeated. "If you blokes can't do what I've paid you for then I'll have to find someone who isn't frightened to take a risk. Someone who's not afraid to step out of their comfort zone."

"I'm not suggesting you quit," Sean replied. "The thing is, Jackson has his permits and council won't back any move to revoke them without good reasons. The Jacksons are a well-respected, established family."

"What about Mandy?" Frank asked. "Isn't she your girlfriend? What does she think about all this?"

"She'll do what I want, if she knows what's good for her," Larry snarled.

"And if she won't?"

"Then I'll dump her."

Interesting News

YOU'LL be my bridesmaid, Mandy, and Steve will be best man. I hope Larry isn't jealous!" Emma grinned as they sat in the Commercial Hotel.

"Who knows." Mandy sighed. "He's in Perth. For a few days, he said, but I haven't heard from him for over a week and he's not answering my calls. I hope he's OK."

"He'll be fine. With Larry it's business first. No doubt he's busy working some deal."

"I wish I was sure," she said wistfully. "I'm obliged for all he's done for me, but . . ."

"Well, you know my views on Larry."

"Yes, and I'm afraid you might be right."

Further discussion was cut short as Brian turned up, followed by Steve. Once again Mandy felt that frisson as he joined them.

Talk went back to the forthcoming wedding before Mandy's phone rang.

"Larry, thank goodness you're all right! I've been worried.

"Yes, I'll come right away."

She excused herself and left.

"I wish she'd see through that man," Emma fretted.

"Not much we can do, Em, if she won't listen to your warnings," Brian said.

"It's not that she won't listen. She feels grateful to Larry and, being a decent person, she tries to see the best in him. But I reckon she's starting to see what he is."

"I hope so. Let's move somewhere more private and have something to eat. I have news and, if it's right, our problems with Larry might be over."

Soon they were in a private room with some of the chef's specials set before them.

"That looks delish!" Emma said looking at Brian's meal. "What is it?"

"It's the coconut-braised Wagyu beef shin with pickled cucumber salad. And you're not wrong, it is delicious."

Steve forking up a mouthful of his Wagyu and mushroom pie.

"My beef is just taking off and now the bank wants to stop me. It's just not fair."

For a few minutes they enjoyed their meals until Emma spoke.

"So, what's this news you've got for us?"

"I went over to Barton to see my sister. She works for the council and I asked what she knew about threats to revoke my permit for the pub redevelopment and Steve's stockyard permit.

"She told me two local government inspectors arrived today. Word is they're investigating several matters including the attempts to revoke our permits. There's also an attempt to fast-track approval for Larry to build a supermarket and shopping centre outside the Whixley Commercial Zone.

"The proposals weren't publicly advertised. Seems Sean McAlpine tried to push them through before any objections could be lodged."

"Lawson's mate," Steve remarked darkly.

"Yes, Lawson's mate. Listen, let's keep this to ourselves for now."

"Any coffees or teas?" the waitress who was clearing the table asked.

"What'll it be?" Brian asked, looking around the table.

"So Lawson's little empire is starting to crack!" Emma commented as the waitress departed to fill their orders.

"Maybe so. But that doesn't solve my problem with the bank," Steve said in a tone of frustration.

"That's true, Steve," Brian said. "But it'll be interesting to see how Paul Robbins and his bank react if the Barton Community Bank opens a branch in Whixley.

"They'd get a lot of business, seeing how unpopular Paul is."

"Mmm. And isn't Mandy's father investigating Paul Robbins and his bank?" Emma concluded.

True Colours

THE more Emma considered Brian's news the more concerned she became for Mandy and what Larry may have involved her in. She was torn between wanting to help her and Brian's wish to keep it quiet.

She rang Brian the following morning and he agreed she should warn Mandy.

"No doubt Larry already knows about the investigations and hopefully they've gone too far for him to interfere!"

Emma then called Mandy and asked to meet up for morning tea.

"We can get some drinks and cake from the coffee shop and sit in the park."

Once they were seated Emma shared Brian's news about his visit to the council.

At first Mandy tried to defend Larry, saying he wouldn't be involved in anything illegal. Then she remembered Frank's warning and told her friend about it.

"I'm scared, Emma. What can I do? I don't want to have to leave Whixley and I don't want to lose my career!"

"Mandy, you have to be strong. You must stand up for what you know is right. Speak to Celia and Carl about the legal side; your friends will know what to do."

"Thanks, Emma. I suppose I've closed my eyes to some of Larry's actions.

"He's been very helpful but now I'm beginning to realise how he's organised my life. That's all very fine while things are going his way, but is it the life I want?"

Mandy frowned.

Yes, he had always been very helpful, but for whom?

She still hesitated to see Larry as other than a hard-nosed businessman, but what if he was a crook? What would this mean for her future in Whixley, and for her career?

The only logical answer was to face up to him and hope that the love she believed they shared would put an end to her fears.

And if that didn't happen? No, she didn't want to go down that track.

Thus she arranged to meet Larry before she lost her nerve.

* * * *

They met in Larry's private lounge at the Railway Hotel. Mandy noticed a half-empty whisky bottle on his desk.

She again shared her concerns about the matters she'd found in Frank's files. She hadn't meant to mention the council investigation but in the end was so worried that it all poured from her.

"Don't worry your pretty little head," Larry

replied smoothly, pouring himself another whisky. "It's all under control. I'll do whatever is necessary to get the results I want."

"But what if that means breaking the law?"

"Let me worry about that," he responded brusquely, downing his drink in one gulp.

When Mandy appeared ready to object he frowned.

"Don't cross me, Mandy. Just trust me."

"Wait, I don't like the sound of that. I'm not your puppet!"

His face hardened.

"Don't fight me, Mandy. I haven't time for that right now. Just shut up and do what I say or you'll be sorry!"

Mandy was shocked. She felt as though Larry had struck her.

Nevertheless she mustered her courage and, with an effort, kept her voice steady.

"What do you mean, I'll be sorry?"

"I mean I'll get Frank to accuse you of stealing. That old fool will do whatever I tell him."

"I thought you loved me! I thought we had a future together."

Mandy's voice wobbled and tears filled her eyes as the truth about Larry finally burned into her brain.

"We do, as long as you don't cross me,"

Larry responded as his phone rang. "I'm busy. We'll finish this later."

Mandy stumbled from the room, her head spinning as she hurried blindly along the street.

What could she do? Was this the end of her career, the end of her time in Whixley?

Somehow she made it back to the legal practice. She slumped at her desk and let her tears flow until there was a quiet knock at her open office door.

"I don't want to intrude, Mandy," Frank said gently, "but it's time we talked."

"Oh, I've been such a fool, Frank!" Mandy sniffed, searching for a tissue to dry her eyes and blow her nose.

"Lawson can be very charming and generous, but when he doesn't get his own way that's another story.

"It's easy to get sucked into his schemes. Very easy." Frank sighed.

While Mandy went to freshen up he made coffee. When she returned he explained how he'd been drawn gradually into Larry's questionable deals.

Finally he showed her a hidden filing cabinet.

"These are my insurance if Larry ever double-crosses me. They reveal the full scope of his activities, including his actions against Steve Jackson and his attempts to gain a monopoly in Whixley by forcing Brian Shelton out of the Commercial Hotel."

"That's terrible, Frank!"

"It is. At first I just bent a few rules, but before long I was breaking them," Frank admitted. "Then I was in so deep I couldn't easily get out.

"My drinking was already a problem and that helped ease my conscience. But really, it's no excuse.

She was hardly able to believe what Frank was saying.

"I'm sorry I got you into this mess, Mandy. Now I have to get you out.

"We must call the Law Institute and report all this so it can be dealt with before you get dragged in and it affects your career."

"What about you? If you reveal these files won't you be in trouble, too?"

"Thank you for your concern, Mandy," Frank replied, courteous as ever. "But it's unlikely I'll be around long enough to be bothered by any trouble.

"The doctors say it's only a matter of months before the liver cancer finishes me. Whereas you have a long bright future and that's what matters."

"I'm so sorry, Frank. I really appreciate you sharing all this with me, but my head's spinning trying to take it all in."

"I understand you need time to get your

head around it all. But we can't wait too long, what with those investigations at the council and the bank.

"It is going to be better if we report all this before it comes out some other way."

"I suppose so." Mandy hesitated.

"Why don't you call Celia and Carl?" he suggested gently. "They're your friends and they'll understand the legalities."

Mandy nodded.

"Emma's already said the same."

Following Frank's advice Mandy rang Celia and then drove down to Melbourne to meet her and Carl after work.

"You're lucky that Frank is prepared to do the right thing," Carl decided when Mandy finished her story. "Without his support this could be very sticky for you."

Mandy stayed with Celia and Carl overnight and first thing next morning she rang Frank.

"Yes, please go ahead and call the Law Institute. And, Frank, thank you again."

"Look after yourself and don't hesitate to call us if you need any help or support," Celia told her, giving Mandy a warm embrace as she was about to leave.

Mandy arrived back in Whixley around eleven and stopped at the store to pick up a few things.

She had just loaded her purchases into her

car when Steve pulled up beside her.

"Hello, Steve. You're looking chirpy today," she greeted him, pleased to see that a wide smile had replaced his worry lines.

It was a smile that, once again, set her heart racing.

"I'm feeling chirpy, and it's all thanks to you and your father," Steve replied. "The bank has overruled Paul Robbins and won't be calling in my loan or Brian's!

"My cattle are coming on nicely and in a month or two they'll be ready for sale. Then I'm going to be able to get all my finances up to date.

"It means now I can get on with my life and rebuild Coolabah!"

"That's fabulous news, Steve!"

They paused for a moment, gazing at each other, both revelling in the good news.

Then, by mutual unspoken consent; they embraced.

The warmth and security of Steve's strong arms lingered with Mandy as she drove out to her house. It was comforting when so much around her was collapsing and threatening her very future.

Street Fight

LATER that afternoon an angry and not entirely sober Larry burst into Paul Robbins's office.

"What's this I hear about Jackson's loan? I thought you had it all fixed to get him off Coolabah and now you say it can't be done!

"Call yourself a bank manager? You're not worth a bank manager's bootlace!"

"Larry, it's out of my hands!" Paul said, his voice quavering under Larry's onslaught.

"Whaddaya mean, it's out of your hands?" Larry demanded.

He was answered by a man he hadn't noticed who had been standing quietly, off to one side, in Paul's office.

"The regional manager has taken over all decisions regarding loans made from this branch."

"Who are you?" Larry turned. "Whaddaya mean by butting in here?"

"Clive Cameron." The man stepped forward and offered Larry a hand. "I'm a Special Bank Inspector and I've been examining loans made from this branch over the last year or two."

"I'm sorry, Larry," Paul mumbled. "He just

turned up and started asking questions."

"Shut up, Paul!" Larry snapped and then glared at Clive. "You're Mandy's father, ain't you?"

"I have that honour," Clive replied calmly, scrutinising Larry.

"Well, Mr Inspector, I suggest you back off and we have a little talk. Unless you want to see your daughter in big trouble."

"Are you threatening me with blackmail?" Clive asked sharply.

"Not threatening," Larry retorted. "Just suggesting that, if you interfere in my business, I'll make sure your daughter's role in the shonky deals done at Frank Barty's practice is exposed.

"And that will sink her career," he concluded maliciously.

"I agree, Mr Lawson. If your allegations were true they would indeed end Mandy's career. But they aren't.

"As we speak Mandy and Frank Barty are talking to officers from the Legal Services Board who are auditing the practice to get the full story.

"In fact, Mr Lawson, your threats are empty."

Larry was taken aback for a second. Then he snapped and, with a roar of rage, launched himself at Clive who nimbly stepped aside, allowing Larry to crash into the wall beside him.

Larry turned to continue his attack but, seeing Clive had adopted a confident boxing stance, he turned and stormed off.

Meanwhile, Clive had got out his phone and had followed Larry into the street.

"Yes, Sergeant, Lawson's just left the bank and he's headed across the street to his hotel . . . oh!"

Clive gasped as he saw his daughter emerge from the legal practice office a few doors along from Larry's hotel.

At the same time Larry saw Mandy and changed direction to confront her.

"Who have you been talking to?" he demanded, grabbing her arm.

"Larry, you're hurting me!" Mandy protested while he continued yelling at her.

Suddenly he swore, let her go and stumbled back, grabbing at the red mark on his face where she'd landed a stinging slap.

"If that's the way you wanna fight . . ." he growled, lunging at Mandy who jumped back.

"Lawson!"

Larry angrily turned towards Steve who had crossed over from the store. He had been loading goods into his battered old LandCruiser when he saw Mandy being attacked.

"Jackson! Whaddaya doing here?" Larry

charged at Steve who danced around, feinting punches and keeping just out of Larry's reach.

His opponent swore and charged about with fists flailing until he was restrained by Sergeant O'Reilly.

"Mr Lawson, you're under arrest," the sergeant said as he handcuffed Larry. "I've been watching you and now I've got you."

"You can't do this!" Larry protested. "What's the charge? You've got nothing on me!"

"We'll start with assault, blackmail, bribery and corruption," Sergeant O'Reilly replied calmly and led Larry away.

"You'll be sorry, Jackson!" Larry yelled. "You think you're so smart but I haven't finished with you yet. You'll see.

"And you, too, Mandy! Don't think you'll escape, either!"

For the second time that day Mandy and Steve were in each other's arms. This time it wasn't just a brief celebratory embrace.

"Thank you," Mandy breathed, nestling into his embrace as her tension drained away. "I was so worried Larry would hurt you!"

"I did some boxing in my younger days," Steve replied, holding her tight. "I was never much good at it but one thing I did learn was that the correct way to fight a big lumbering opponent is to stay out of their reach, while they exhaust themselves charging around."

"You must think me such a fool. Emma tried to warn me but I didn't listen."

"Not at all. Larry's quite a charmer until he can't get his own way. Naturally you felt indebted after all he did for you."

"Ahem." Clive coughed politely. "Sorry love, I have to leave you, but I see you're in good hands. I've some unfinished business with a soon-to-be-ex-bank manager."

Clive returned to the bank where Paul was still slumped on his desk, holding his bowed head in his hands.

Mandy and Steve continued to hold each other.

"How can I ever thank you?"

"How about we start with dinner tonight," Steve replied. "And we get to know each other better. Eh, cuz?"

"I can't think of anything I'd like better," Mandy replied.

New Beginnings

ALL'S well that ends well." Brian smiled at Emma, Mandy and Steve on Friday evening when they gathered for a celebratory dinner at the Commercial Hotel.

"Yeah, but I wouldn't want to go through any of it again!" Steve commented. "Although one good thing has come out of it," he conceded, smiling at Mandy.

"I always knew you two were meant for each other. Now we can have a double wedding at Easter!" Emma cried.

"I think we need to take things slowly for a while. There's only so much change a girl can cope with at once!" Mandy laughed.

"Talking of change," Emma continued, "is it true that you're taking over the Whixley Legal Practice?"

"It is. Frank surrendered his Practising Certificate. He wanted to just retire and give me the practice but I insisted on paying him a fair price.

"After all, he put his neck on the line for me and I had that compensation money from when I was wrongly dismissed."

"That's fabulous, Mandy," Emma responded. "Now we're both going to be sole practitioners. Making a real difference for real people."

"Well, I may not be a sole practitioner for long." The words popped out before Mandy could stop them.

"Don't tell me Steve's planning to study law?" Emma grinned.

"Not me," Steve answered. "I'm a farmer, not a student."

"Who, then? You can't keep us in suspense," Emma insisted.

"Nothing's finalised yet so please don't say anything. It's just that Celia and Carl are talking about moving to Whixley.

"She wants to get out of the city rat race, especially with a baby on the way, and Carl realised he could commute to Melbourne from here as easily as he could from the suburbs."

"That is great news!" Emma replied. "Let's drink to new beginnings."

When the toast was finished Brian informed them all that Sean McAlpine, the council planning officer, had been suspended and had been charged with corruption.

"So I don't think Steve and I have to worry about our planning permits any more."

Sabotage!

MANDY and Steve spent every spare minute together building their relationship. Both could relax knowing that Larry and his cronies were being dealt with.

On Thursday afternoon they were leaning against the stockyard fence and planning a weekend in Melbourne.

"We'll drive down tomorrow afternoon and meet Celia and Carl at their place after work," Mandy decided. "Celia's booked a table at a really good restaurant nearby."

"Sounds great," Steve replied with a contented sigh. "I can hardly believe how quickly things have changed.

"Larry's off my back and you're in my arms," he concluded, drawing Mandy close for a long kiss.

As they parted a silver station-wagon with red government number plates entered the yard.

"It's probably some lost public servant," Steve remarked.

He went forward to greet the driver, a stocky, pleasant-faced man who was dressed in smart work clothes and wearing well-polished, elastic-sided work boots.

"Steve Jackson?" the driver asked.

"That's me. How can I help?"

"I'm Ross Martin, District Veterinary Officer with Agriculture Victoria."

The man flashed an official ID.

"I'm following up a report that cattle from your property appear to have eaten contaminated feed, making their meat unfit for human consumption."

And just like that, despite Steve's protests Coolabah was placed in quarantine, meaning no cattle could be brought onto, or removed from the property.

"It's just until we know how the cattle-feed became contaminated and ensure the problem is solved," Ross told him.

"Just when everything seemed to be going so well!" Steve lamented. "Now I'm back to square one."

"I'm sorry. We'll try to sort it all as soon as possible. My staff will be here in the morning to do some tests," Ross informed him before he collected some feed samples and drove off.

Steve slumped against the stockyard fence.

"I'm sorry, Mandy, but this puts paid to our weekend away. If I can't buy or sell stock I won't be able to keep up with my loan payments and I'll still lose Coolabah.

"I may as well give up."

"Don't you dare. We'll beat this

together," Mandy affirmed with more confidence than she felt. "First we should call Emma and get her professional advice, then we'll phone the police."

"I'll be there in an hour," Emma promised after they had done this.

"Meantime, let's look around and see if we can find anything that might give us a clue as to how this happened," Mandy said.

She and Steve began to inspect the property.

A few minutes later he pointed to where a cigarette butt had been stubbed out in a corner of the feed shed.

"That's strange," he remarked. "Someone's been smoking here. Lucky the idiot didn't burn the place down."

"Don't touch it, Steve," Mandy cautioned as he went to pick it up. "It could be evidence of who has been here."

"And this is interesting," she added, bending down to look at a driver's licence that was lying on the floor nearby. "Do you know this fellow?"

Steve hunkered down to examine the photo on the licence.

"Looks like that shifty character I saw with Lawson the other day."

As he stood up sudden understanding lit up his face.

"Now I know what Lawson meant by

those threats when he was arrested."

Sergeant O'Reilly and Emma both arrived about an hour later to examine the scene, collect evidence and take photos.

"This one's a petty criminal I've had my eyes on for a while," the sergeant told them when he saw the licence.

"This young fellow will lie to you like a pig in straw," he observed, putting the licence in an evidence bag. "But I think he'll sing like a canary when we put this to him and he's facing gaol time. And that'll give us another thing to help put Lawson away."

"But it doesn't help my situation," Steve mourned. "I still have to find the money to pay my debts and loan."

Emma collected samples from the stockyards and feed shed, where she found several bags of feed had been tampered with.

"I'm sorry, Steve, but it appears someone has either tried to poison your stock or, at least, contaminate them. I'll know more when I've had these samples tested."

Mandy and Emma both tried to encourage Steve but he seemed to have lost heart.

He didn't even react when Sergeant O'Reilly pointed to a partly burned candle he'd found under an inverted bucket.

"Look at this; someone's been trying to burn your shed! Lucky it went out before the fire took hold."

Sergeant O'Reilly left shortly afterwards, promising to have a Crime Scene Investigator there in the morning. Emma was called away soon after to see a sick horse.

Left alone, Mandy and Steve sat together on the homestead veranda, grateful for the cool evening breeze.

Even in this second week of February the late summer days were still topping 30°C.

Later, when Mandy produced plates of steak and chips with salad, Steve ate heartily despite previously claiming he wasn't hungry.

"Sorry, but I have to go," she said around nine. "I've got to prepare some paperwork for a client I'm seeing first thing tomorrow."

"That's OK. I feel much better after talking to you and knowing your father will speak to the bank for me. Don't know what I'd do without you."

Although he put on a brave face, deep down Steve still couldn't help feeling this was the end for the Jacksons at Coolabah Flats.

Reunited

BY the time Mandy completed her paperwork and took her nightcap out to the veranda it was past midnight.

She gazed across the valley at Coolabah, illuminated by the full moon. She wished she could help Steve but her funds were all committed to her house and purchasing the law practice.

Her thoughts drifted to Ian Jackson, her ancestor, who'd left Coolabah over 120 years ago and had died on the other side of the continent. Then her gaze drifted down to the creek where the ruins of the burned shed stood stark in the bright moonlight.

Could the answer to Coolabah's problems possibly lie in that ruin? She couldn't shake away the persistent thought.

She finished her drink and went inside, but instead of going to bed she began rummaging in Aunt Clara's trunk.

As if by destiny she picked up an old, handwritten sheet that had slipped down beside the newspapers. Her excitement mounted as she read the partly written letter from Ian Jackson to his parents.

It was dated June 1897, the month before he died.

Ian explained his need to prove himself and not play second fiddle to his brother.

He apologised for any worry he'd caused his parents, assuring them he was well and telling them about his marriage, his expected child and his successful gold claim.

Mandy's eyes nearly popped out of her head as she read on.

I'd been hiding some of the gold from our Coolabah Mine, planning to take it as my share of the inheritance.

In the end I only took a few ounces and buried about 100 ounces in a strongbox under the back left corner of the new shed by the creek.

"So you'll be able to pay off all your debts!" Mandy told Steve in a phone call first thing next morning.

"Provided it's still there," Steve responded, hardly daring to think his problems were solved.

* * * *

Two weeks later Mandy and Steve, Emma and Brian and Celia and Carl were at the Annual Dinner Dance to support the Whixley Fire Brigade and State Emergency Services Unit.

As usual it was held in the Soldier's Memorial Hall.

"So, when's the big day?" Emma asked as

they settled down for their first course.

"Emma McLeod, you are a shameless matchmaker," Brian told his love, grinning broadly.

"Well, somebody has to give those two a push. They're made for each other."

"Shall we tell them now?" Mandy asked, turning to Steve.

"I guess they have to know sometime," he replied with a grin

"Ta-da!" Mandy exclaimed.

She held out her left hand to show the diamond ring sparkling on her third finger.

"Wow, Mandy! Congratulations"

"Well, now that Steve's debts are all cleared we're thinking the Queen's Birthday weekend in June," Mandy told them. "That will give Steve time to tie up any loose ends regarding the contaminated cattle-feed and he'll be able to get Coolabah ready for me to move in."

"But what about your house?" Emma wanted to know.

"Ah! That's Celia's good news." Mandy looked at her friend.

"Carl and I have decided we are moving to Whixley and we're buying Mandy's house.

"I'll work part time with Mandy after the baby is born and Carl can easily commute to Melbourne."

"That's not all," Mandy said. "I'm going to be wearing Great-aunt Clara's wedding gown, the one we found in the trunk. It just needs a little alteration.

"At last it will see the two branches of the Jackson family reunited."

The End.

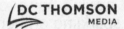

Published in Great Britain by DC Thomson & Co. Ltd., Dundee, Glasgow and London. Distributed by Frontline Ltd, Stuart House, St John's St, Peterborough, Cambridgeshire PE1 5DD. Tel: +44 (0) 1733 555161. Website: www.frontlinedistribution.co.uk EXPORT DISTRIBUTION (excluding AU and NZ) Seymour Distribution Ltd, 2 East Poultry Avenue, London EC1A 9PT. Tel: +44(0)20 7429 4000. Fax: +44(0)20 7429 4001. Email: info@seymour.co.uk. Website: www.seymour.co.uk.

© DC Thomson & Co. Ltd., and David Kippen, 2022.

DON'T MISS THE NEXT POCKET NOVEL NO. 960, ON SALE MARCH 3, 2020.

IF YOU ARE LOOKING FOR BACK NUMBERS PLEASE TELEPHONE 0800 318846